GHOST SAVE THE QUEEN

GHOSTS OF LONDON 3

NIC SAINT

PUSS IN PRINT PUBLICATIONS

GHOST SAVE THE QUEEN

Ghosts of London 3

Edited by Chereese Graves

www.nicsaint.com

Give feedback on the book at: info@nicsaint.com

facebook.com/nicsaintauthor
@nicsaintauthor

First Edition

Printed in the U.S.A

CHAPTER 1

"What do you think, Elvis? Add this statuette to our little pile?"

Elvis stared at his compadre, then allowed his gaze to drift down to the statuette in question. It depicted an Olympic wrestler, all bulging muscle and awkward poses. He lifted his massive shoulders in a shrug. "Sure. Why not?"

He might not like the figurine, but that didn't mean someone else mightn't. As a professional burglar, he subscribed to the philosophy that robbing a place was not unlike creating a sales funnel: the more you dumped into the funnel, the better. Later on, when you paid a visit to your designated fence, he'd be the one to sift and sieve and select those precious nuggets that made it all worth your while. In other words, it didn't behoove him to be choosy in this, the burglarious stage of the proceedings. Now it was about filling up that funnel and fill her up good and plenty.

"Let's get a move on," he told Chuck, his partner in crime. "We haven't got all night." He hoisted the sports bag onto his shoulder. It made the delightful rattling sound a bag full of stolen goodies makes. Music to his ears.

"What do you reckon?" asked Chuck, a gaunt scrapper with a goatee.

"What do I reckon what?" he asked, checking around.

"Do you reckon we've got everything?"

Elvis looked around the living room. "Did you take the TV?"

"Yup."

"The stereo?"

"Yes, sir."

"Laptops, smartphones, computers and other junk?"

"Took it all, sir."

"Then I think our work here is done, Chuck."

"I love to hear you say it, Elvis."

He wiped a bead of perspiration from his brow and grunted contentedly.

What the novice in the burgling trade often underestimates is the stress involved in this often maligned business. Even though in these days of social media you can be relatively sure a homeowner will be out of the way, as you can track their whereabouts on a minute by minute basis, you're never a hundred percent sure. In Elvis's extensive experience, burgling houses worked best when owners were out. For some reason, they tended to cavil at their hard-earned stuff being unceremoniously stolen from under their noses.

Nathan Livermore, whose house they were now visiting in an unofficial capacity, had been so nice as to post on his Twitter that he and his wife and daughter were guests at a reception hosted by the Conservative Party. Mrs. Livermore had even shared a seemingly endless stream of pictures on her Instagram, indicating the Livermore family was having a whale of a time.

Social media had heralded in a new era for burglars across the globe. Never before had it been easier to know if a house was ripe for burgling, people so anxious to tell the world what they were up to and where. Of course, you had to consider that some of these posts were nothing more than mere posturing. It wouldn't be the first time that he and Chuck had to haul ass when a homeowner returned home unexpectedly even when his Facebook feed indicated he was still across town whooping it up and having a great time with the boys. People simply couldn't be trusted these days, could they?

But so far so good. He'd just checked his phone, and Mrs. Livermore was too busy showing off her new Stella McCartney to hurry home. And he was just grabbing another sports bag, this one filled to the brim with designer clothes and expensive Savile Row suits, when a softly spoken request reached his ear. It sounded a lot like, "Stand me a drink, will you?"

Instantly, his eyes swiveled to Chuck, but the latter was checking the row of family pictures on the credenza in Nathan Livermore's study and hadn't spoken. Elvis had often stressed the need for silence on the job, Chuck being a relentless blabbermouth who couldn't keep his trap shut for five minutes.

But the sound had come from the liquor cabinet in the corner, and his heart jumped up into his throat, colliding with his uvula. Could it be that the Livermores had entered through the backdoor? If so, they were in trouble!

"Did you hear that?" he hissed, his eyes narrowing into tiny slits.

"Hear what?" asked Chuck, picking up a picture of Pia Livermore.

"There's someone here," he whispered, gesturing at the liquor cabinet.

Chuck looked over at the spot indicated. "I don't hear a thing."

Just then, a whiny voice exclaimed, "Just pour me a drink already."

This time Chuck heard it, his next words confirming this. "I heard it, too."

And it was then that the figure emerged, walking straight through the study wall behind the drinks cabinet, slightly rattling the bottles on display and the neat set of expensive tumblers. It took Elvis a few seconds to realize what was wrong with this picture. As a rule, people don't walk through walls, or at least not in his experience. If he could walk through walls, he'd have tried it a long time ago. It would have saved him the trouble of having to learn how to jimmy doors and pick locks.

"Um, Elvis?" asked Chuck. "What's going on?"

"I have no idea, Chuck," he said. Apart from the fact that the newcomer had entered the room in such an unorthodox fashion, he appeared to be slightly luminescent, as if he'd been taking regular baths in that funky glow-in-the-dark paint the makers of that *Avatar* movie were so obviously fond of.

"Just fix me a drink," said the guy, evidently fond of harping on the same theme. "My throat is parched," he explained, gesturing at his vocal instrument. To Elvis's surprise, there was a long gash in his throat, as if it had been slit from ear to ear with a very sharp instrument for some reason.

"No wonder it's parched," chuckled Chuck. "There's an 'ole in it!"

"I know that," snapped the guy. "Someone didn't like the way God created my throat and decided to make improvements in the shape of a slot."

Elvis gulped. In all his years as a breaker and enterer of other people's homes he'd never experienced something quite like this. It disconcerted him a great deal. "So what happened to you?" he asked now, a little lamely perhaps.

"Like I said, they went to town on my throat, and I haven't had a drink since. So could you do me a favor and fix me one? I can't seem to do it."

"Why?" asked Chuck. "I mean, why don't you do it yourself? Or are you one of them anonymous alcoholics who are not allowed to touch the stuff?"

The guy stared at Chuck for a beat, then slowly said, "Not exactly. After having my throat slit, I died, you see, and one of the drawbacks of being dead is that you don't get to enjoy the simple little pleasures in life. Like drinking."

"So you're... you're dead?" asked Elvis, just to be sure.

"Afraid so," said the guy with a rattling sigh that emanated in equal parts from his lips and the gash in his throat. A light spray of blood accompanied the sigh and Elvis gulped again, this time in disgust. Sweeney Todd might have enjoyed the spectacle, but he sure as heck didn't. "I used to live in this house," continued the dead guy. "Well, I still live here, of course, but now I'm forced to share the space with the Livermores." He lifted his chin, which only served to widen the bloody red chasm beneath it. "My privacy, which I've always valued dearly, has been seriously hampered, I don't mind telling you."

"I can see that," said Elvis.

"Yeah, I wouldn't like it either if my 'ouse was overrun with squatters," added Chuck cheerfully. The sight of the dead guy didn't seem to affect him the same way it did Elvis. But then again, Chuck had a ghoulish streak. He was a great fan of horror movies, and every Halloween liked to dress up as Count Dracula, fake fangs and liters of fake blood and all.

The newcomer thrust out his hand. "Where are my manners? My name is Noble Dingles. So nice to meet you."

"Pleasure I'm sure," said Chuck, also holding out his paw

in an attempt to shake the other man's hand. Instead, he miscalculated and shoved it right through him, which momentarily gave him pause. "That's weird," he said.

"What's your name, my friend?" Noble asked, addressing Elvis now.

"Elvis Presley," said Elvis, after Chuck's experience settling for a wave.

Noble Dingles's eyebrows rose a fraction of an inch. "Elvis Presley? But you don't look anything like the King."

"He doesn't, does he?" asked Chuck with a laugh. "And you haven't heard him sing. Trust me, he doesn't sound anything like the King, either."

Elvis threw his associate a look of censure. "I'm not *the* Elvis Presley."

"Not unless you're dead like me," agreed Noble. "And I would know if you were. One of the perks of being dead is that you can easily spot a faker."

"My dad thought he was doing me a favor when he decided to call me Elvis," he grumbled. "I still don't get what's so funny about it, though."

"I do," said Chuck cheerfully. "It's hilarious."

"Well, it certainly is a very remarkable name," said Noble amiably. "Have you ever considered going into showbiz?"

"I told you," said Chuck, shaking with mirth now. "Elvis can't sing."

"Nor do I want to," said Elvis with a glowering look at his partner.

"And what's your name, sir?" Noble asked.

"Chuck Berry. Like the singer."

For a moment, the ghost seemed lost for words. "How about that?"

"And I can't sing either!" Chuck laughed loudly.

That was true enough. What Elvis and Chuck had in common were fathers with a very weird sense of humor, but whatever their intentions had been, neither Chuck nor Elvis had ever had any singing ambitions. Or at least Elvis hadn't. Unlike most people, he'd found his aim in life at a very young age, when, prompted by his friends, he'd stolen a butter ball at his local sweet shop and had discovered he had a talent for absconding with things that weren't necessarily his. It had led to a long and lucrative career.

Which reminded him. "If you're dead, then what are you still hanging around here for?" As far as he knew—and of course this was only secondhand knowledge—when you were dead you either went up or down. Up to heaven or down to hell, depending on whether you'd been good or bad.

"I don't know," said Noble. "For some reason I seem to be stuck here."

"Do you know who killed you?" asked Elvis. The situation reminded him of that Patrick Swayze movie, where his ghost couldn't move on until he'd solved his own murder, and made sure his wife wasn't being harassed. Maybe this guy had a pretty wife like Demi Moore tucked away somewhere, and he needed to save her from the guy who now played the president on *Scandal*.

"No, actually I don't," admitted Noble. "I mean, I saw his face and all, but I don't know who he is. Never saw him before, which struck me as absolutely unfair. Who goes and kills a perfect stranger?"

"Maybe he was a terrorist?" suggested Chuck. "Terrorists like to kill strangers. They get a big kick out of it, for some strange reason."

"I don't think so," said Noble, rubbing an absentminded finger along the gash in his throat. "He didn't strike me as a terrorist. He didn't have that crazed look in his eyes. No, my killer was very cool and poised." He pointed at his cut throat. "And professional. See what he did? Nice, clean cut."

"Yeah, looks like the work of a professional if you ask me," said Chuck.

"He's not asking you, Chuck," grumbled Elvis, who didn't like all this talk about bloody gashes. He was squeamish that way, and didn't like blood. It was one thing he liked about his profession: there was no killing involved.

"Oh, but actually I *am* asking you," said Noble. "You can't imagine how nice it is to finally be able to chat with someone. What are you doing here, if you don't mind my asking? Are you guys friends with the Livermores?"

"Um, not exactly," said Elvis.

"We're thieves," said Chuck. "We're here to rob the Livermores blind."

"Chuck!" hissed Elvis. "You don't need to tell him that!"

"Oh, but it's perfectly all right," said Noble. "I don't mind. Nathan Livermore is such a boor, and his wife such an absolutely unpleasant person. And don't even get me started on that bratty teenage daughter of theirs."

"Don't like the new owners much, eh?" asked Chuck.

"As a matter of fact I don't. I've been doing my best to scare them off, but they're very persistent. Simply refuse to budge so far."

"They can hear you?" asked Chuck, interested.

"Well, they can hear me knocking. And still they appear unfazed."

"Hey, maybe they'll blame you for the burglary," said Chuck.

"Oh, I'm sure they will," Noble agreed.

"They just might," Elvis admitted. Which was just great. "If they blame the burglary on you, I'm pretty sure they won't call the cops."

"I wouldn't be too sure about that," said Noble, offering the discordant note. "They're pretty matey with Scotland

Yard. Livermore went to school with some inspector called Watley, so I'm sure he'll be the first one he calls."

"You won't tell on us, though, right?" asked Chuck.

Noble Dingles grinned. "Of course not. I just hope this proves to be the straw that broke the camel's back and they finally pack up and leave. And speaking of camels, I have a small suggestion for you gentlemen. Do you see that horrible painting residing so imperiously over Livermore's desk?"

One hour later, as Elvis and Chuck dumped their nice little haul on the floor of their van's cargo hold, Chuck said, "That was pretty weird."

"You can say that again," Elvis agreed, shaking his head. As he walked around the van and opened the door, he darted a final look back at the house and saw that Noble Dingles was watching their departure with interest, and even gave a little wave. He waved back, and then quickly climbed inside the cabin and shoved the key into the ignition. "Weird, but very rewarding."

"Extremely rewarding. I think the boss will be happy."

"I think he'll be over the moon."

"Pity we couldn't stand the guy a drink, though."

"Pity," he agreed. They'd tried to pour Noble a stiff one, but the amber liquid had simply trickled right through the ghost and ended up on the floor.

"Nice fellow, too. Great conversationalist. And," he added, putting his feet up on the dash as the van lurched away from the curb, "great to know there's life after death. In our profession it's good to know that death ain't the end."

And then they were driving away. Elvis wondered how Nathan Livermore would react when he discovered that his most prized possession was gone. It was possibly the greatest haul they'd ever gotten their hands on, and they owed it all to Noble. "I just hope the poor guy gets his house back."

"I hope so too."

They both sighed. They might be crooks, but they had a sentimental streak, and loved to see justice done. It just didn't do, Elvis felt, for a nice guy like Noble to have his house stolen from under him. Even if he was dead.

CHAPTER 2

*D*arian was dreaming of spending a nice, leisurely vacation on some tropical island with Harry McCabre when he got the call. They'd just lain down in their hammock, preparatory to some serious necking, when he was roused from sleep by that blasted cell phone. He turned around with a tired groan and picked it up. "Watley," he growled, none too friendly. He listened for the space of a few seconds, then announced, "I'll be there in ten minutes."

He rose from the bed and spent thirty precious seconds of the ten minutes he'd allotted himself rubbing the sleep from his eyes and wondering why they would call him in for an ordinary burglary. But then Scotland Yard switchboard operators aren't always known for their perspicacity, and it was with an agonized groan that he lifted his bulk from the bed and proceeded to get dressed. He was a powerfully built man with a shock of dark hair and penetrating gray eyes, a battering ram of a chin and the chiseled features so prevalent amongst Scotland Yard's finest. Five minutes later, he was racing along the deserted London streets, wet from the light drizzle that was falling.

He arrived there in exactly four minutes, and thirty seconds later he was entering the house. Constable Tilda Fret, a heavy-set woman with flaming red hair, was already on the scene, and so were a bunch of other officers, which was perhaps a little surprising for a mere break-in, but he didn't ask questions. He'd socialized with Nathan Livermore, and knew that the man was one of England's most promising young politicians, and even rumored to be the next mayor of London, and perhaps even a future Prime Minister.

He found Livermore in the kitchen, clasping a cup of tea. He was a tall, floppy-haired man with a goofy expression on his face and an easygoing manner. Not quite what one would expect from a politician. His wife Nicolle, seated beside him, looked haggard and drawn, their daughter Pia red-faced. It was obvious both women had been crying, and perhaps so had Nathan.

"So what happened?" he asked, pulling up a chair and taking a seat.

"They took everything," said Nathan brokenly. "Absolutely everything."

"What did they take, exactly?"

"Mum's engagement ring, for one thing," said Pia, rubbing her eyes.

He stared at Nicolle, an attractive woman with braided auburn locks. "The, um…" He didn't know how to pose the question in a way that wouldn't sound awkward, so he decided just to blurt it out. "The expensive one?"

The woman nodded. "Yes."

He blinked. "That stunning fifty million quid sparkler?"

She nodded again, a lone tear slipping down her cheek.

He had to suppress an urge to whistle through his teeth. If the thieves had gotten hold of Nicolle's engagement ring, they'd gotten away with a nice haul.

Apart from the monetary value, there was the emotional

value the ring represented. It had once belonged to Nathan's great-aunt, who was one of the Queen's favorite cousins and best friends, and had caused quite a stir when her late husband had offered it to her in exchange for her hand in marriage. As such, some said it should be part of the Crown Jewels, and kept at the Tower of London and not be part of the private collection of a commoner like Nicolle Livermore. Dubbed the Pink Eulalie, the ring's 60-karat diamond was something of a rarity. One of the world's most expensive stones, in fact.

"You kept it at the house?" he asked.

"It was in the safe in my study." He shook his head. "I don't know how they managed, because it's supposed to be theft proof, but they cracked it."

Five minutes later, they were in the study. The moment the door was closed, Nathan turned to him and said "This is a nightmare, Darian."

He'd come to that conclusion himself already. The Pink Eulalie was a unique gem. Even though reportedly valued at fifty million, the truth was that it was priceless, and he was sure the Queen, notified of the loss of her favorite cousin's ring, would have a few choice words to say on the matter.

"It's not just the ring. It's much worse than that."

"Worse? How can it be worse?"

Nathan walked over to the safe, which was concealed behind a portrait of the man's mother guarding over the politician's desk. It was one of the more ghastly paintings in Nathan's possession, a rather hideous portrayal of the matronly woman, but apparently not enough of a deterrent to keep the burglars at bay. The painting swung open on its hinges, and revealed the safe door, which was ajar. "They took my great-aunt's last will and testament," said Nathan, indicating the empty safe. His voice shook with emotion.

"So?" asked Darian. "I can't imagine a mere piece of paper will fetch them a great deal of money."

"There were certain... stipulations contained in the will," said Nathan, his voice dropping an octave. "Certain stipulations only I was privy to. And now the world will know about those, too."

"The underworld, you mean," he said, but shut up when Nathan gave him a look of such profound agony he felt inclined to place a reassuring hand on his friend's shoulder. He walked over and did so now. "What was in the will?"

Nathan hung his head. "A deal Victoria made with Conservative Party leadership."

"What was the deal?"

"To appoint me the next Prime Minister." He looked up, and added, miserably, "And lead England out of the European Union once and for all."

Darian's jaw dropped. "What?" he asked, not believing his own ears.

Nathan nodded. "My great-aunt Victoria has always been very keen on England regaining its independence and not being at the beck and call of those bureaucratic Brussels butchers. She felt it incumbent upon her to put someone in charge who would make this dream a reality in the near future."

"But if word gets out there will be a scandal the likes of which this country has never seen!" Darian cried. "This will be bigger than Profumo!"

Nathan nodded miserably. "It might herald in the end of our monarchy."

Darian stared at the man. He could hardly believe this was really true. "So you're supposed to be the next Prime Minister?" he asked his friend.

"Yes, I am," said Nathan. "First they were going to make me Mayor of London, grooming me for the top spot. This has all been arranged years and years ago. It takes time to put all the players in place. Like a game of chess."

"This all sounds very much like *House of Cards*, Nathan."

"Within a democracy there's only so much you can do," Nathan explained. "There are certain limitations you need to consider. Constraints."

"Like the popular vote," he said, shaking his head.

"Well, yes. But that can be manipulated, of course."

"What can be manipulated?" suddenly a voice asked from the door.

Darian and Nathan both looked up in horror. Darian hadn't heard the door opening. He was even more surprised when he saw that it was Harry McCabre, looking at them both with a curious look on her pixie face.

"How did you get in here?" asked Nathan, visibly perturbed.

Harry shrugged. "I was invited by your wife. Me and my colleagues."

"Is she one of yours?" asked Nathan.

Darian considered the question. "Well, not exactly," he said finally.

And she didn't look a police officer, of course, with her jeans jacket, mussed-up blond bob and shiny golden eyes, alive with the light of intelligence. She walked up to Nathan now, hand outstretched. "I'm the ghost hunter your wife hired. To get rid of the poltergeist that's been bugging you?"

CHAPTER 3

*I*t had already come as something of a surprise to
Harry that when she arrived she found the place
swarming with police officers. She couldn't imagine they'd
all been brought out here to deal with the poltergeist. As far
as she knew ghost hunting wasn't part of the Scotland Yard
mission statement.

She'd gotten an urgent phone call just after one o'clock,
confirming the tentative arrangement she'd already made
with Nicolle Livermore. This time, the woman said, she
needed to get rid of the ghost and get rid of it right now.

Apparently this poltergeist had been making strange
noises for the last couple of months, leaving ectoplasmic
spots on the couch, raiding the pantry in the middle of the
night and generally making an absolute nuisance of itself.

When finally she and her small crew arrived on the scene,
the police hadn't even allowed her to set foot on the
premises. It had taken an executive order from Nicolle Livermore herself to get access to the scene of the ghostly crime,
and even then she couldn't get any of the officers to discuss
what had taken place here at this late hour, nor could she get

an interview with the lady of the house, as she was being interviewed by Constable Fret.

So she'd idly roamed the house, wondering where the ghost might be, and enduring curious looks from the cops, who seemed to feel she was like that thing they'd just found crawling out from under a flat stone in the garden.

Finally, she'd arrived at the study, and had just happened to overhear Nicolle's husband—at least that's who she assumed the weary voice belonged to—discuss something rather sensitive and personal with Darian.

Darian's eyes, already widened to their maximum possible dilation after Nathan's revelations, widened even more when they perceived that their conversation, which apparently he'd assumed was of a private nature, had been overheard by a third party. The third party being his girl-friend Harry.

She gave Nathan Livermore, a man who looked like a young Hugh Grant, a kindly smile. "Has this got something to do with the poltergeist?"

"None of your business," growled Livermore, giving her a vicious scowl.

She sighed. She saw what was going on here. Nicolle Livermore had probably forgotten to inform her husband she was calling in the Wraith Wranglers. It was often that way. One member of the family believed in ghosts, and called in the ghost hunters, while another member didn't believe in ghosts, and as a consequence was vehemently opposed to the presence of any ghost hunters. It was very much a case of the left hand not knowing what the right hand was doing, or, as in this case, a husband not knowing what his wife was up to. It was difficult to work like this, but she was used to it.

"There's a ghost in your house, Mr. Livermore, and your wife has hired us to get rid of it."

"My... wife? Hired you?" asked Nathan, incredulous.

"Yes, sir. She feels that only a professional can dislodge this ghost—poltergeist is the technical term—so she called in my team and me."

"Your... team?" asked Nathan, adopting the modus operandi of a parrot.

At this moment, Jarrett walked in. "This place is a dump." Then he caught sight of Nathan and gave him a little wave of his pinky finger. "Oh, hi, Nate. Didn't see you there. Great place you've got here. Real snazzy."

"This is my team," said Harry. "Or at least part of it." She would have clarified that an actual ghost was also a member of the team, but for some reason had the impression this wouldn't go over well with Mr. Livermore.

"What are you doing here, Zephyr?" growled the beleaguered politician.

"I was called for," said Jarrett affably. "By your wife. Not in that way, of course," he quickly added when he realized his words might be misconstrued. "I wouldn't touch your wife if she was the last woman on earth and I was the last man. Not that she's not a very attractive woman," he hastened to say, "because she is. But if there was anyone I fancied it would be you, if you see what I mean. Not that I do fancy you, of course. As if!" he added with a light chuckle. "Don't you go getting any ideas now, you hear? Ha ha."

Nathan frowned, and judging from his next words, Jarrett's little speech hadn't allayed his concerns or quelled his animosity. "I should have known you were into ghost hunting these days. Always chasing the latest fad, eh?"

"Well, if you can call ghost hunting a fad. I like to consider it a noble service to mankind, and in that sense I'm treading in the footsteps of illustrious men like Mother Teresa and Princess Diana. So where is this pesky little ghost of yours, Nate? I mean, where have you seen him last?"

"I don't know what you're talking about. There are no

ghosts in my house, except in the imagination of notorious attention whores like yourself."

"Me and your wife, you mean," said Jarrett, "who also believes in ghosts, judging from her urgent missive to lend her aid in this, her hour of need."

"Just get the hell out of my house!" yelled Nathan with cracking voice.

"Um, you might want to reconsider, Nate," said Darian now.

Nathan stared at him. "Don't tell me you believe in ghosts, too!"

Harry knew that Darian had been in the same position as Nathan Livermore. He, too, had been a skeptic, until a ghost had slimed him. It had left an indelible impression, and since the incident he'd joined the camp of the staunch believers, though he was obviously reluctant to share this new allegiance with the world, his Scotland Yard colleagues, or his friends.

"I, um…" said Darian. "I'd like you to meet my, um, my girlfriend, Nathan." He gestured at Harry. "Her name is Henrietta McCabre."

"Just call me Harry," said Harry magnanimously. "All my friends do."

She was pleased as punch that Darian had introduced her as his girlfriend. Other, weaker, men, might have hesitated to come to the defense of a ghost hunter, especially to their longtime friends, but not Darian Watley. She felt Nathan Livermore measure her up, clearly seeing her in a different light now. Not only did she have the endorsement of his wife, but also of the Scotland Yard man on the scene.

"Pleased to meet you, Miss McCabre," he finally said. "But that doesn't alter the fact that I want both you and your associate out of here at once."

"Miss McCabre and Mr. Zephyr-Thornton are staying

put," suddenly a voice piped up from the door. The study was quickly turning into a meeting of Parliament, with MPs arguing back and forth over the minutest trifle. The woman who'd just entered was the lady of the house, and she was staring daggers at her husband. She quickly made her meaning clear. "I hired Harry and Jarrett to take care of our ghost problem and that's exactly what they will do. Do you know how hard it is to get an appointment?"

That was true enough. Ever since they'd started advertising, their workload had increased tremendously. Not that Harry minded. Since the antique store she'd inherited was sold this was her only job, and she was devoted to helping people with the gift she'd discovered she had. The gift of getting in touch with the dead, and helping them move on to the great beyond.

"You can't be serious," said Nathan, exasperated. "Ghost hunters? Really?"

"You know as well as I do that we need to handle this ghost business once and for all," she said sternly. "I don't want to have this poltergeist crawling all over the house. It's extremely trying, and especially hard on Pia. She can't concentrate on her studies, and she can't even invite her friends over because each time she does this poltergeist makes a perfect nuisance of itself. Besides—I'm sure that the ghost is responsible for this burglary."

"That's simply ludicrous!"

"How else did they get into your safe, Nathan? Tell me that."

Nathan darted a quick look at this friend. "I'm terribly sorry about this, Darian. Perhaps we can continue our discussion at another time."

Darian nodded, which reminded Harry that Nathan still hadn't answered her question. "So what can be manipulated?" she asked now.

Nathan gave her a very nasty look. He obviously didn't want her butting into what he seemed to feel were his private affairs.

Darian cleared his throat. "I think we've taken up enough of Nathan and Nicolle's time already," he said. "They've been through a terrible ordeal tonight, with the burglary and all, and I think it's time to let them have—"

"I'm sorry, Darian, but I beg to differ," said Jarrett. "I don't know about you, but we're here to do a job and that's exactly what we're going to do."

"Now look here…"

And while Jarrett, Darian and Nathan were engaged in a lively discussion, Harry drifted toward the safe and saw it was completely empty. Nicolle had assured her that the safe was impregnable, and couldn't be burgled without someone knowing the combination, and she was convinced the ghost that haunted their house had something to do with this. She wondered now what, exactly, had been stolen that was so important to drag her and Jarrett out of bed in the middle of the night, and thought it had something to do with the conversation she'd inadvertently overheard.

Something about the Queen of England, and this being the end of the monarchy. She wondered what exactly could have been in the safe that would form a threat to the monarchy. She knew better than to press Nathan to tell her what was going on, though. They were here to find and chase away a poltergeist, not to solve a burglary. That was Darian's task. So she turned to Mrs. Livermore and spirited her most chipper expression on her face. The one she reserved for clients having been scared witless by a spook.

"So where have you seen this ghost last, Mrs. Livermore?"

CHAPTER 4

"*I*'m one hundred percent certain this burglary has something to do with the ghost," said Nicolle, after they'd settled down in the parlor. Police officers were still flitting to and fro, dusting surfaces for fingerprints, checking the floor for footprints and doing whatever it was that police officers usually did.

"What makes you say that?" asked Harry.

Nicolle wrung her hands, visibly distraught. She was sitting ramrod straight, her pale face betraying her extreme agitation. "I've been hearing its voice," she finally declared, after a brief struggle with herself, then shivered.

"Voice?" asked Jarrett. "What kind of voice, Nicolle?"

"Oh, Jarrett," she said, and suddenly a lone tear slid down her pale cheek. "You know the kind. Cajoling us, taunting us, urging us to go."

"What does it want, exactly?" asked Harry, leaning forward. This was a very important point. The sooner they knew the poltergeist's motive, the sooner they could make contact and try to figure out how to get rid of it.

Nicolle raised an ineffectual hand. "Well, he says he's thirsty."

"So it's a he, is it?" asked Jarrett.

"It has a male voice," confirmed Nicolle.

"And he's thirsty?" prompted Harry.

"Yes. Very thirsty. Parched is the word he uses, and he accuses us of invading his territory, taking over his house... denying him what he wants."

"A drink," supplied Jarrett. "Well, I can understand that. It's not much fun being a thirsty ghost, I can imagine. That's a spot you can't touch. Not when you're dead, if you see what I mean."

"He has no business here," Nicolle said primly. "This is our house, where I want to live in peace with my family. Where I want to see my daughter have a happy time, just like any child, and allow my husband to go about his business undisturbed. Did you know that we can never have any friends over? Because of this ghost we've been forced to live here under siege."

"What happens when you invite someone?" asked Harry. She had a pretty good idea what would happen, but wanted to hear it from Nicolle.

"He scares everyone off that he doesn't like, which seems to be every living person. He makes a mess of things. The last party we had was Pia's birthday party. Her sweet sixteen. She'd invited her friends over, quite a lot of them, as you can imagine, and then this poltergeist, or whatever you call him, decided to have some fun by turning everyone's clothes inside out."

"He did what?" asked Jarrett with a light chuckle.

Nicolle gave him a stern look. "It wasn't funny! All of their clothes were turned inside out, while they were still wearing them. Their... brassieres were on top of their under-garments, on top of their shirts. And their knickers... Well, I don't have to draw you a picture. It wasn't pretty. Especially for poor Clementine, who was just having her, well, her time of the month. Bloody awful, the whole thing was, and extremely traumatizing as they all blamed Pia for playing a trick on them, even though she had nothing to do with it."

"It must have been terrible," said Harry consolingly.

"Pia lost a great deal of friends over the debacle. It disturbed her greatly, so we decided not to invite anyone over as long as that… thing is here. And that's when I decided to call in, well, you," she said, gesturing at Harry.

"What strikes me as odd is that this ghost has been here all this time but only decided to start raising Cain these last few months," said Harry.

"Yes, that's very odd indeed."

"How long have you lived here, exactly?"

"Three years, and the first two of them were absolutely blissful."

"The ghost never made itself heard?"

"Never. Not a peep."

"I wonder what triggered these events," said Harry musingly.

"I'll bet he was still getting used to his new situation," said Jarrett. "You often see this type of behavior when ghosts are still fresh," he explained. "They just died and don't understand what's going on. When finally it dawns on them what happened they hope against hope that the situation is reversible. They hang around the morgue, visit their grave, and generally try to get to grips with the situation. And since time for ghosts is measured differently than it is for us, it might take them a few months or even years to finally accept that this is their fate and that they're pretty much stuck here."

"And that's when they often start to make a fuss," said Harry.

"They act out. Exact revenge on the living," added Jarrett.

"Do you have any idea who this ghost might be?" asked Harry.

"Probably the previous owner," Jarrett said.

Nicolle stared at them. "The previous owner?" she asked.

"Yes. Did you know him?" asked Harry.

Nicolle looked away, then slowly shook her head. "No. Everything was arranged through the agency."

"They didn't tell you what happened?" asked Harry.

"Well... he told us the previous owner died, but no specifics."

She suddenly seemed distracted, and Harry had the feeling she wasn't telling them something.

"Didn't the neighbors tell you?" asked Jarrett. "Usually they're more than keen to supply that kind of information, especially in cases of violence."

"Violence?" asked Nicolle, staring at Jarrett. "What do you mean?"

"Ghosts usually have gone through such an experience," explained Harry. "That's why they're incapable of moving on. They can't come to terms with the way they died, and want to solve their own murder and see justice done."

"Or they simply forgot to turn off the gas oven and don't know they inadvertently caused their own demise," said Jarrett with a grin. "Not all ghosts are blessed with the kind of intelligence you and I take for granted."

"He keeps asking for a drink," said Nicolle distractedly. "A stiff one."

"Why would he help burglars burgle your house?" asked Harry.

"That's obvious, isn't it? He wants to cause us harm, and now with my engagement ring gone..."

Jarrett whistled through his teeth. "The Pink Eulalie? They took it?"

She nodded, then fixed them with an imploring look.

"Please chase away this poltergeist. And make him return my ring. I don't care about the rest."

Harry and Jarrett shared a look of determination, and Harry said, "Rest assured, Mrs. Livermore. We're going to get to the bottom of this."

"Yes, the Wraith Wranglers are on the case," said Jarrett earnestly.

"Thank you," she said, eyes swimming with tears. "Thank you so much."

"We'll kick some serious ectoplasmic butt," Jarrett added for good measure.

Nicolle glanced at Jarrett a little uncertainly. She seemed to feel he was, perhaps, hard to take seriously. But finally she held out her hand and shook Harry's. "You've got yourself a deal, Miss McCabre."

"Harry, please," she said, pressing the woman's hand warmly.

CHAPTER 5

*F*ats Domino was thinking hard, tapping his finger on his desk. He was a swarthy, dark-haired man of considerable bulk and hairiness. Once again he was trying to come up with a way to find the money to pay for his little girl's treatment. Doctors all over the country had given up on her, declaring her brain tumor inoperable, and had given him to understand he should simply accept the unacceptable: that she wasn't going to make it. He'd found a specialist in Boston who was experimenting with a new technique. But the treatment would cost an arm and a leg. Money he simply didn't have.

Just then, the gate of the small garage box he kept in Soho clattered open, and his two associates clambered in, carrying bulky sports bags.

"Finally," he grumbled, rising to his feet with an effort.

"Sorry, boss," said Chuck. "We was held up."

"What did you get?" he asked. He'd had high hopes for this job, as the Livermores were well-off and rumored to possess quite a nice bit of art. But when Elvis held the biggest damn ring under his nose he'd ever seen, he stared at it, not believing his eyes. Even in his wildest dreams... "But that-that-that's the Pink Eulalie!" he cried. "You mean they kept it at the house?"

"Yes, they did, the suckers," confirmed Elvis with a wicked grin.

He knew all about the Pink Eulalie but, like everyone in the business, thought the Livermores kept it locked up in a bank vault somewhere.

He picked it up and stared at it, marveling at the sheer size of the rock. "Absolutely amazing," he gushed, his eyes sparkling as much as the stone. But his smile quickly vanished and he placed it on the upturned oil drum that served as his reception desk. "What else have you got?" he asked brusquely.

Elvis and Chuck shared a look of confusion. "But, boss. That's the Pink Eulalie! That must be worth a pretty penny, huh? What do you reckon?"

"Nothing!" he cried. "This blasted stone won't fetch us a bloody dime!"

Elvis's face fell, and so did Chuck's, and he turned away from his two associates to hide his disappointment, then kicked at an old exhaust pipe. This was his place of business, and the place where he fixed up old cars.

"So it's a fake?" asked Elvis. "Should have known it was too good to be true."

"And here I thought it was the real deal," said Chuck, disappointed.

"It *is* the real deal," said Fats, returning to the oil drum to pick up the famous ring once again. It really was remarkable. Sixty karats if you please!

"I don't get it, boss," said Elvis. "I thought this ring was supposed to be worth fifty million smackeroos?"

"Yeah, that's what I heard. Fifty million smackeroos," echoed Chuck.

"The Pink Eulalie *is* worth fifty mil," he confirmed, "if only we could sell it. Unfortunately this particular rock is so bloody famous that nobody will touch it with a ten-foot pole! None of our regular people will come near it!"

"Maybe a private collector?" suggested Elvis. "There must be someone out there who wants this ring and is willing to pay through the nose for it."

Fats gave him a look of exasperation. "And how do you propose we find this private collector?"

"We ask around," suggested Chuck. "Keep our ear to the grindstone."

"The ground," muttered Elvis.

"What's that?"

"You don't keep your ear to the grindstone, you dumbass. You keep it to the ground."

"I don't care what you do with your ears, but I keep them to the grindstone," said Chuck haughtily. "Which is what I'll do right now."

"Keep your ear to the grindstone and it'll be ripped clean off!"

Chuck shrugged. "Your ears maybe," was his only comment.

"Just shut up, you two," Fats ground out. He wagged a finger in Chuck's face. "Don't breathe a word about this rock to anyone, you hear?"

"But how are we supposed to ask around?" asked Chuck, surprised.

"We don't, you idiot!" cried Fats, whose frustration was mounting. They had the most famous stone in the country, maybe even the world, and they couldn't shift it without attracting a lot of unwanted attention.

"Why don't we ask Master Edwards?" suggested Elvis, referring to the well-known crime boss. "He's usually well-informed. And well-connected."

"He's also well-retired," Chuck pointed out.

"Not for a score like this, he's not."

"I'm sure that if word gets out we've got the Pink Eulalie, Edwards will simply try to get the stone for himself, and leave us empty-handed," Fats muttered, thinking hard. He needed money to pay for his little girl's operation, and this stone was just the kind of miracle he'd been hoping and praying for. Elvis was right, of course. If they could only find a private collector who'd add this trinket to his collection, no questions asked...

"Let's sleep on it," Elvis finally said, unusually sagacious.

"That's what my mother always used to say," Chuck chimed in.

"What else have you got?" asked Fats, gesturing at the sports bags.

Chuck dumped the contents on the oil drum, and he checked it. There was a nice silver cigar case, a bunch of rings and bracelets, three gold watches... All stuff they could easily find a buyer for.

"There's more stuff in the van," said Chuck.

"Yeah, a neat flatscreen, a couple of laptops, iPads, iPods..."

Fats's eye fell on an envelope and he snapped it up. "What's this?"

"Just something we found in the safe, Fats," said Elvis.

He quickly opened it, having no qualms about reading another person's private letters. He quickly scanned the document, which looked official, with lots of signatures and stamps and stuff. "Last will and testament of... Victoria Smelt." He frowned. The name rang a bell, but where had he heard it before? Smelt, Smelt, Smelt... And then he got it. The Queen's favorite cousin, who'd died a couple of years ago at the ripe old age of one hundred and one. And as he read on, struggling with the legalese, he finally gave up. It didn't matter. He remembered now. At the time the papers had been full of it. Dame Victoria Smelt had promised her grandnephew he'd be the next Prime Minister if he promised to lead the country out of the European Union.

"Listen," he said, waving the document enthusiastically. "Say, listen."

"We're listening," confirmed Chuck.

"Say, listen," he repeated, his cheeks flushed now from excitement. "This document... It's the bee's knees. The cat's whiskers. I mean, this is it!"

Chuck and Elvis shared a quick look. They obviously thought he'd gone off the deep end. "The bee's knees, Fats?" asked Elvis. "What's in the will?"

He tapped the document smartly. "It's the Smelt will!"

Chuck sniffed. "I don't think so, Fats. Doesn't smell."

Elvis also sniffed. "I detect a slight whiff of perfume."

"Not smelled, Smelt! Victoria Smelt! The Queen's cousin! Don't you remember?! All that to-do a couple of years ago when the old dame died? Everyone said she made arrangements for Livermore to become the next Prime Minister and liberate us from those pesky Brussels bureaucrats!"

"Oh, if only that were true," said Elvis wistfully. Like most Britons he thoroughly disliked Brussels telling him not to use his old toaster, get rid of the old-fashioned light bulb and replace it with those terrible LED lamps that gave off such a cold, unnatural light and prohibited the composting of teabags. Not that he ever did compost his teabags, but it was simply the principle of the thing. You simply don't tell an Englishman where to put his teabags.

"So it's all right there in the will?" asked Chuck.

"I have no idea," he confessed. "But I'm pretty sure it is."

"Which means..." Elvis prompted.

Fats grinned from ear to ear. "Which means good old

Nate will pay through the nose to get his hands on this document, boys."

Elvis frowned. "You mean you want to blackmail the guy?"

"Of course! He won't want this here document to fall into the hands of the Daily Mail or The Sun! He'll pay us whatever we want, I'm sure."

"But we've never done blackmail before, boss," said Chuck.

"Yeah, blackmail is an entirely different ball of wax, boss."

"I don't care. This is where the money is, laddies. This is where we make our big score." He picked up the stone. "And while we're at it, why not sell him back his ring?" He grinned. "This is the one. This is the big score we've all been waiting for. The big moola!" And judging from the smiles that now lit up the plug-ugly mugs of his associates, they were as enthusiastic about the prospect of netting a couple of million smackeroos as he was. So he clapped their shoulders with relish. "You did good, boys. You did great!"

"Thanks, boss," said Elvis.

"Yeah, thanks, boss," echoed Chuck. "So how much are we netting?"

"Millions!" He thought about the smile on his little girl's face when he'd tell her the good news. At long last, after all the hardship they'd gone through, the sun was finally breaking through the clouds.

"Maybe we should reserve some of that money for Dingles, Elvis."

"Yeah," confirmed Elvis. "Good idea, Chuck. We should get him some."

He frowned. "Dingles? Who the hell is Dingles?"

"Noble Dingles. He's the ghost that helped us open the safe," Elvis said.

"He was very thirsty," said Chuck. "But he can't drink, on account of the fact that he's a ghost. Terrible ordeal, that."

"Terrible," Elvis agreed, licking his lips and darting a look at the fridge.

"What are you talking about?" asked Fats. "What ghost?"

"Well, there was a ghost," Chuck explained, "who was very thirsty, cause someone's gone and sliced his throat."

"Mean cut, boss," Elvis added with a grimace. "Real mean cut."

"We owe him, see? He told us about the safe. Gave us the combination."

Fats's frown had deepened and he now burst out, "Ghosts don't exist, you morons!"

"Oh, but they do, boss," stressed Chuck. "We saw him as clearly as we see you. Didn't we, Elvis?"

"We sure did, boss. And it wouldn't be fair not to share the loot with the guy. After all, without him we wouldn't be having this nice windfall."

There was a momentary silence, while Fats wondered whether his men had gone completely mental or merely soft in the head. It was certainly possible. He'd seen it happen before when the stress of the job became too much. Guys could go barmy in this highly competitive profession of theirs.

Now was not the time to come unstuck, however. They needed to launch a very delicate blackmail operation, fraught with even more danger than burgling the place in the first place. So he held up an appeasing hand. Just humor them, he told himself. They might be barmy, but at least they were still functioning. When all this was over, they'd never have to do another job again. He'd simply cut them loose and that would be the end of it.

"All right," he said now. "You wanna help this Dingles?

You help Dingles. But it'll have to be from your cut, all right? Leave me out of it."

"All right, boss," said Elvis.

"Yeah, it'll be our way of paying it backward," said Chuck.

"Paying it forward, you numbnuts," growled Elvis.

"That's what I said."

"No, it wasn't! You said—"

"Whatever, crooner. We'll pay this ghost from our cut. It's only fair." Chuck grinned. "I'll bet it'll be a hoot. We never worked with a ghost before."

"Yeah, I'll bet," said Fats vaguely. He was starting to think that maybe—just maybe—he should cut these two losers loose right now. He could pocket the proceeds of the transaction, and have these two idiots properly sectioned.

CHAPTER 6

*T*he police officers had finally all left the house, and so had the Livermores, who were going to stay with a friend while Harry and Jarrett tried to root out the poltergeist. It had taken some persuading for Nathan to agree with this unusual arrangement, as he didn't like the idea of the Wraith Wranglers chasing a ghost in his freshly burglarized house, but finally he'd relented, and now Harry and Jarrett had the house to themselves.

"Why is that, actually?" Harry asked as they went from room to room, trying to get in touch with the specter who'd deemed it necessary to try and chase away the Livermores.

"Why is what?" asked Jarrett as he held up the new contraption he'd bought from Amazon. The device, which looked like an electrometer, supposedly could detect the presence of spectral mass, but so far hadn't given a beep.

"Why does Nathan Livermore dislike you so much?"

It was something she'd asked herself from the moment it became clear the two men weren't too keen on each other. She knew that Jarrett was something of an acquired taste, and even though she loved her friend and found him hilarious, at times she had to concede he was a little... crass.

Jarrett chuckled. "That might have something to do with the fact that I once pelted him with an egg."

"You pelted him with an egg? Why would you do a thing like that?"

Jarrett shrugged, waving his spectermeter. "When you're boys in boarding school together throwing eggs is just one of those things one does. Although I must admit they were usually boiled eggs. I made the mistake of picking a nice, fresh one, and managed to seriously mess up Nate's costume."

"Do you think he remembers?"

"Oh, yes, he does. One doesn't forget one's first egg-pelting incident. He was an egg virgin up to that point, which probably explains a lot."

It didn't really explain anything, but Harry decided not to press the point.

"You have to understand that Nate's family has ties to the Crown, and as such I've always considered it my sacred task to bring him down a peg or two. Make sure he doesn't get above himself, if you see what I mean. And eggs feature largely into such a scheme. In a sense I think the incident gave him backbone. So he probably should be grateful. Not that he is, mind you. He seems to feel I owe him one, which just goes to show I shouldn't have limited myself to just the one egg. To permanently fix a conceited ass like Nate Livermore requires more than one soft-boiled egg. Two, perhaps, or even three." He shook his head. "If only I'd known then what I know now."

"Well, you can always try hitting him with an egg again," she suggested.

He smiled. "The suggestion certainly has merit, Harry, and I appreciate the endorsement, but somehow I don't think that's such a good idea. He might retaliate by stringing me up in the Tower of London or something, or have me deported to some black site where they still practice waterboarding. From a guy who's destined to become the next PM you can expect anything."

"Do you really think he's going to be our next PM?"

"It wouldn't surprise me. Nate's an exceedingly ambitious man."

"I wonder what he and Darian were discussing. Did you know those two were friends?"

"I don't doubt it. A person in Nate's position can always use a copper on his list of friends and associates. He's an avid networker, that man is." He rattled his spectermeter and finally shook his head. "This thing is worthless." Then he turned to Harry. "So Nate and Darian were having a chat, eh?"

"In Nathan's study. I barged in just when he was saying something about the Queen and the end of the monarchy. The last thing I heard was he needed to manipulate something. Or someone."

Jarrett mused for a moment. They were now in the living room, and had doused all the lights, creating the perfect atmosphere for the ghost to put in an appearance. Ghosts don't like the light, as it reminds them too much of the bright lights at the end of the tunnel they have to pass through on their way to the other side. "Well, Nate is the grandnephew of Victoria Smelt, who was one of the Queen's favorite cousins. It is rumored she drew up a will that outlined some sort of shady deal with the Conservative Party to boost Nate's political career, though its stipulations were never made public, of course.

"The fact that he was in such a tizzy indicates this document might have been amongst the haul the burglars got away with. If it was indeed Victoria Smelt's will, and Nate is talking about manipulating people, there's a good chance something in La Smelt's will smelled funny, if you catch my drift. Some deep, dark secret that might affect the monarchy."

"Which may explain why Nathan was so upset," said Harry, nodding. If some secret document was stolen from his safe, he'd want it back even more than the Pink Eulalie, which was, after all, merely a diamond ring.

"This loot," she said now. "They can never hope to sell it, can they? I mean, the Pink Eulalie is so famous that no regular jeweler will touch it."

"Trust me, Harry, there will always be people interested in buying a Pink Eulalie," said Jarrett. "I'm sure they'll have no trouble finding a buyer."

She gave him a curious look. "How come you know so much about it?"

"Well, I know for a fact that some of the items in the Zephyr-Thornton collection haven't necessarily been obtained through the proper channels."

"Your dad was a thief?" she asked, flabbergasted.

"No, not dad," he said with a chuckle. "The old boy would never stoop to theft. But some of the Zephyr-Thornton ancestors have. How else do you think they amassed such a vast fortune and an art collection that would make any museum curator salivate? In the olden days it rarely happened that fortunes were created through aboveboard means. I'm sure there was a lot of boiling oil, the use of morning stars and more than a few catapults involved, not to mention a small army of bloodthirsty knights and other scurvy knaves. Make no mistake, darling, pillaging goes a long way to acquiring wealth."

"Well, I just wonder…"

But what she was wondering would never be known, for at that moment Jarrett heaved a loud curse. "What a piece of crap," he muttered, referring to his spectermeter, not to the fortunes of his forefathers. "Oh, ghosty," he said now. "Oh, ghosty, where art thou? Come out, come out wherever you are…"

"Maybe we should simply open a bottle of wine?" suggested Harry. "Nicolle did mention how he's always asking for a drink."

"Excellent idea," said Jarrett. "I could use on myself." He switched on the light and walked over to the drinks cabinet. He seemed to know his way around Nathan's house quite well, and when Harry said as much, he said, "I have attended a few parties here, it's true. Nate and I may not see eye to eye, but that doesn't mean I don't manage to weasel my way in from time to time."

She shook her head as he took another drink. "Leave some for the ghost."

"But of course." He held out his tumbler, the amber liquid sloshing invitingly, and said in a singsongy voice, "Oh, ghosty. Where are you?"

Still there was no response, but Harry had a feeling it wouldn't be long now. If this ghost was really as parched as he always said he was, he wouldn't be able to resist a shot of the very best, as she guessed Nathan's stock was.

Then, suddenly, she thought she detected movement from the corner of her eye, and as she whipped around, was just in time to see the shape of a man drifting in through the wall. And as she watched in fascination, she wasn't surprised to see that he had a bloody gash where his throat used to be.

When the newcomer spoke, the sound seemed to come as much from this second mouth as the first, which was disconcerting, even for a veteran ghost hunter like herself. "Where's that drink?" he croaked. "I'm parched!"

CHAPTER 7

"*R*ight here, big fella," said Jarrett as he held out the beaker with the golden nectar. The new arrival wasn't a 'big fella', though. He was rather on the smallish side, with long, curly gray hair and a hook nose that stuck out of his face like a sun dial. He looked like a nobleman, albeit a pint-sized version.

Jarrett held the glass in front of the man's prominent nose and the ghost sniffed eagerly. Then he attempted to take it from Jarrett's fingers but failed. The moment Jarrett let go of the tumbler, it tumbled to the floor and the precious liquid was spilled on one of Nicolle's nice carpets. The ghost let rip a cry of agony as he watched the liquor being soaked up by the carpet and so did Jarrett, who also strongly felt alcohol belonged in a glass, not the floor.

"Dammit," Jarrett growled.

"You took the words right out of my mouth, my friend," said the ghost as he knelt down and tried to lick the carpet. For a moment, Harry expected Jarrett to get down on all fours himself and join the ghost in his efforts to salvage the liquor, but he seemed to feel it was below his dignity.

Besides, there was a lot more where it came from, so he simply returned to the liquor cabinet, poured himself another drink and slung it back in one gulp.

"Aaaaah," he said, licking his lips. "That hit the spot."

The ghost stared up at him with visible dismay. "I wish you wouldn't do that," he lamented.

"Do what?" asked Jarrett innocently, toying with the empty glass.

"It's not nice to taunt a ghost, Jarrett," Harry said reprovingly.

"Well, it did the trick, didn't it?" he asked softly.

"Why can't I have a drink?" asked the ghost plaintively.

"Because you, my dear friend, are dead," said Jarrett, rubbing it in.

"I know I'm dead," grumbled the ghost. "But why can't I have a drink? That's not too much to ask for, is it? Just a teensy-weensy little drink."

"Actually, it is too much to ask for," said Harry gently as she took a seat on the sofa nearest to the ghost, who was still on the floor. "You see, once you pass over to the other side, you don't have a physical body anymore, so you can't interact with the physical universe the way you used to when you were still a part of it."

"I know all that," said the ghost petulantly, as he plunked himself down on the floor. "But that doesn't mean I have to like it, does it?"

"No, indeed it doesn't," Jarrett agreed. "What's your name, my friend?"

The ghost stared at him, none too friendly, but finally relented. "Noble Dingles. What's yours?"

"Jarrett Zephyr-Thornton the Third," he said, the words easily rolling off his tongue.

"That's a mouthful," muttered Dingles.

"And I'm Harry," said Harry, even though no one had

asked her. "Well, actually it's Henrietta, but everybody calls me Harry. Harry McCabre. And we're here to help you, Mr. Dingles," she explained.

"Help me do what?" asked the ghost, who was obviously in a foul mood.

"Help you make sense of this new reality," she said kindly. She'd often felt it was much easier to work with a ghost when first she established some kind of rapport. Ghosts were human, after all, and liked to be treated as such. Even though they could be a genuine pain in the behind, a lot of them were very nice once you got to know them a little better.

"I don't need your help," said Noble. "I'm perfectly capable of taking care of myself, thank you very much."

"I'm sorry to disagree, old boy," said Jarrett, "but from what I heard you've been making quite a nuisance of yourself, which tells me you need help."

"I'm not a nuisance," said the ghost testily. "This is my house. I can do whatever I want and nobody can tell me differently. Not in my own house."

"It's not your house anymore," Jarrett pointed out. "So there's that."

"As long as I live here, this is my house," he insisted. "And whoever thinks they can muscle in have got another thing coming. It's called trespassing, and I don't like trespassers any more than the next guy."

"But you're dead now, see?" asked Jarrett. "And the living have precedence over the dead when it comes to such matters as ownership."

The ghost shrugged and lapsed into a moody silence.

"The thing is, the people who live here now, the Livermores, would very much like to talk to you," said Harry, whose approach was less confrontational than Jarrett's. She preferred it that way. She'd never gotten results from antagonizing the dead, and she sometimes wondered if this bad cop approach by Jarrett actually worked.

"The Livermores are a horrible bunch," said the ghost, finding speech again. "And the sooner they leave *my* house, the better off they'll be."

"They're never going to leave, buddy," said Jarrett. "They bought the place, for a hefty sum I would imagine, and they like to call it home now."

Noble shrugged. "I'm sure they'll soon clear out." He grinned as he gestured at the now empty walls where the flatscreen had hung, and Nicolle's carefully selected expensive artwork. "Hard to call this a home now, isn't it?"

"Did you have something to do with this burglary?" asked Harry now.

He grinned, his smile, like his cut, stretching from ear to ear. It was a horrible sight, as if the ghost had two mouths, and didn't know from which mouth to speak. "I might have," he said. "I might have given them a hand."

"But why would you do that?" asked Jarrett, who, like any rich person, disliked those positioned lower on the income scale to steal from him.

"Isn't it obvious?" asked Harry. "Mr. Dingles wants to chase the Livermores away. This robbery serves his purpose exactly, isn't that right?"

"It certainly does," agreed Noble. "Look, we can sit and chat all night, and I appreciate the conversation—just like I enjoyed the conversation with the other guys, but at the end of the day this is my house, and there's nothing wrong with clearing out the stuff that doesn't belong here. I'm very happy to have been able to assist Chuck and Elvis with a few helpful pointers."

"Like the combination of the safe?" asked Harry.

"Certainly. I've watched Livermore open that safe countless times."

"You shouldn't have done that," said Jarrett, shaking his head. It was rare for him to be upset. He was probably the most unflappable person Harry knew. But he probably had a safe at home, and so did his father, and to think that ghosts were now cooperating with the criminal classes to rob the upper classes blind was no doubt a dreadful prospect.

"You really don't want to do this," Harry agreed. "It's not very nice."

"I already have," he said, "and I'd do it again in a heartbeat. Nathan Livermore is a boor and a nuisance and so is his wife and that bratty daughter of theirs. The sooner they're gone, the sooner I can go back to my old life and start getting on my feet again. And finally have that drink."

Even though Noble knew he was a ghost, there were some aspects of the ghostdom that seemed to escape him. Like the fact that there was no going back once you were dead. He still seemed to feel that this was a passing phase, and soon he'd be a living, breathing person again, living in his own home, just like before. These 'intruders' weren't going away, and neither was he going to magically come alive again.

"Noble, you're dead now," said Harry gently. "You're never going to be alive again. You're never going to return to your old life, no matter how hard you try. And the sooner you accept that, the sooner you'll find peace."

He stared at her, visibly upset. Then, with a loud growl, he suddenly reared up from the floor, and snarled, "You're a liar, Harry McCabre!"

"Hey, that rhymes!" said Jarrett.

"No, it doesn't," muttered Harry, slightly alarmed at the vehemence with which the ghost had spoken.

"I'll get you out of my house," growled Noble. "Just you wait and see. I'll get you all out of my house, the whole lot of you!"

And with these words, he suddenly flashed through Harry, then through Jarrett, and then disappeared into the wall. It was a strange sensation, and not one that Harry particularly liked, especially when she discovered that Noble had left a good deal of slime on her person. In fact she was covered in it, from head to toe, and so was Jarrett.

"My nice suit!" Jarrett groaned, dripping with the stuff. "It's ruined!"

"At least now we know how Darian felt when he got slimed," Harry said, spitting out some of the slime and wiping big globs from her eyes.

"I'd say our first mission was a bust, Harry."

"I'd say you're right, Jarrett."

He sighed. "One for the ghost... nil for the Wraith Wranglers."

CHAPTER 8

"The Pink Eulalie, one of the most expensive gemstones in history, was stolen last night from the home of Nathan Livermore, the well-known MP for the Conservative Party," the ITV newscaster intoned gravely. "Its theft is a devastating blow to Nicolle Livermore, née Tart, who received the ring in the Livermore shock engagement nearly two decades ago. Denizen of the wealthy Livermore family and grandnephew of Dame Victoria Smelt, Nathan Livermore is rumored to be the next mayor of London…"

"Shock engagement?" asked Jarrett, sitting up in bed. It was his habit of a morning to watch some light breakfast TV while still ensconced in his four-poster bed in the suite he kept at the Ritz-Carlton. Deshawn Little, his manservant, took this time to discuss the day's itinerary and lay out some suitable clothes for his master, and then set about preparing breakfast.

"Excuse me, sir?" asked Deshawn, a stocky man of indefinite age with thinning brown hair.

"What's all this about a shock engagement, Deshawn?"

Even though Jarrett was a boyhood chum of Nathan's, he

didn't remember there being a great to-do about his wedding to La Tart.

"I presume it's in reference to the fact that Mrs. Livermore used to be what they call a call girl, sir," said Deshawn. "Also known as an escort or a working girl." He held up two shirts now. "The pink one with the purple stripe or the butter-yellow twill with the blue monogram, sir?"

He motioned at the one on the left. "Pink, Deshawn. I feel very pinkish today, I don't mind telling you. Especially after the kind of night I had."

"Very trying, sir?"

"Exceedingly. I was slimed, Deshawn, if you have to know."

"Indeed, sir?"

"Indeed. By a ghost who wouldn't play ball, as the Americans are so fond of saying."

"A terrible ordeal, I'm sure, sir."

"It was. I didn't know slime tasted like sewage, Deshawn, and smelled like it, too."

"I wasn't aware of that, sir."

"Well, now you are, so try not to get any of it into your mouth, Deshawn. It is not a fun experience."

"I'll keep it in mind, sir."

"So good old Nate married a call girl, eh?"

"Indeed he did, sir. The engagement made quite a splash."

"You don't say."

"Oh, but I do say, sir."

"So he called her and they hit it off, eh? That's his story and he's sticking to it?"

"It would appear so, sir."

"I didn't even know Nate was into the saucy stuff. If I'd known I'd have pelted him with a few more eggs when the pelting was good."

"Will you require the slimed suit to be dry-cleaned, sir?"

Jarrett gave his assistant a cold look. Deshawn Little wasn't merely his manservant but also his chauffeur, confidant and constant companion. He was even part of the Wraith Wranglers team, though last night he'd been unavoidably detained, due to a social function at his club.

"No, just throw it, Deshawn," he said. "I never liked it much anyway."

"As you say, sir."

"Have you ascertained the identity of Nate Livermore's ghost?"

"Yes, sir, indeed I have. Noble Dingles was a civil servant, in the employ of the Ministry of Defense."

"Must have been some civil servant, if he could afford a place like that."

"It appears he inherited the house from a favorite aunt, sir."

"Oh, he did, did he?" asked Jarrett musingly. "And how did he die?"

"Throat slit by an intruder, sir," said Deshawn dispassionately.

"Nasty business, that."

"Yes, sir."

"Did they ever catch this throat-slitting intruder?"

"No, they did not, sir. The miscreant was never caught."

"Quite a blot on Darian Watley's reputation, that. When was this?"

"Three years ago, sir."

"Yes, that's what Nicolle said. I wonder if we can't solve this murder and rid the Livermores of this pesky ghost once and for all."

"That would be most judicious, sir," agreed Deshawn.

"So now we're in the crime-solving business, eh?" asked Jarrett, liking the idea.

"It would appear so, sir."

"Well, if Sherlock Holmes could do it, why can't we, right?"

"Right, sir. Might I make the suggestion you confer with Detective Watley, sir? He might have more information on the case."

"Yes," mused Jarrett, getting out of bed and straightening his pink pajamas. "We better take Darian into our confidence if we want to succeed."

"He is dating Miss McCabre, is he not?"

"He is," said Jarrett, brightening. "Let's sign the man up for our team."

"A great idea, sir, if you don't mind me saying so."

"I don't mind at all," said Jarrett, heading for the bathroom.

And as he splashed around in the bath, enjoying a vigorous back scrub from Deshawn with the new back scrubber he'd picked up at Harrods the other day, he thought this latest endeavor was probably the most fun he'd ever had with any activity he'd ever engaged in. He'd run a space program at one time, before the spaceship had crashed in the Mojave Desert, had tried his hand—or rather his feet—at figure skating, had been a candidate on Celebrity Big Brother, had tried to break Richard Branson's hot air ballooning record, had been a rock star and even a Taekwondo hopeful. But this ghost hunting thing was by far the most challenging thing he'd tried his hand at. And so far he wasn't bored, which was always a good sign.

"Thanks, Deshawn," he said when his back was glowing. "That'll be all."

"As you wish, sir," said Deshawn in his mellifluous voice, and left the scene stage left to attend to Jarrett's breakfast.

And as he lay back amongst the cherry blossom scented bubbles, he allowed his mind to drift back to the conversation Harry had overheard between Nate and Darian. Something about the end of the monarchy. He didn't like that. He liked the monarchy just fine, and so did the majority of Britons. If the documents this 'Chuck and Elvis'—fake names, he was sure of it—had stolen were to cause the monarchy embarrassment or irreparable damage, they must be found immediately. Then again, a bit of trouble had never done anyone any harm. It could only serve to remind Britain's population of the importance of the monarchy. Strengthen the allegiance. Just like an inoculation gave you a little bit of the flu, a minor scandal might even be a good thing. Get rid of complacency and all that stuff. Remind people not to take a good thing for granted.

It had been quite a while since they'd had a nice little scandal dominating the front pages of the tabloids. Perhaps Noble Dingles had done them all a favor by allowing those secret documents to be stolen. And as he played with the plastic duck that was his favorite toy in the bath, allowing it to pop up after dunking it in the soapy water, he thought perhaps it wasn't such a bad idea to take things a little further. If Nate wasn't talking, and neither was Darian, because of some silly stipulation in the Scotland Yard man's contract not to spill the beans to the general public about things discovered on his watch, perhaps they simply could ask Noble Dingles what was going on.

No doubt the ghost would know perfectly well what was in this mysterious document. And as he descended briefly beneath the hot soapy water, allowing it to close over his head, he thought he'd found the trick to making this silly Dingles do their bidding: pronounce themselves firmly in his camp. That would make the slime-spewing spook think twice.

CHAPTER 9

*H*arry woke up and stretched luxuriously. Her cat Snuggles was purring up a storm. Harry had gotten home late last night, and forgotten to check the snowy white Persian's bowl. Probably she was all out of kibble. Snuggles followed the same routine every day: during the night, she liked to take up space at Harry's feet, but as soon as light came peeping through the curtains, she came snuggling up to her, pressing her nose in the crook of Harry's neck.

The moment Harry stirred, she started softly meowing, urging her to get up, and start her day, and she wasn't happy until Harry had finally thrown off the blankets and gotten out of bed. She did so now, for she saw that she'd overslept. She had arranged to have breakfast over at Em's place, and she was late already. Em was Darian's mother, and a good friend of Harry's. She lived in the apartment next to Darian, so they saw a good deal of each other.

She placed her feet on the floor, rubbing the sleep from her eyes, and then pushed her shaggy blond hair from her face. Oh, God, she needed a shower badly. Last night she'd simply rinsed off most of the slime, but had been too tired to do a good job. She'd dropped into bed and had fallen asleep before her head even hit the pillow.

It had been quite a night, and even though she should be used to chasing ghosts by now, having been in the ghost hunting business for a couple of months now, the wispy breed still managed to surprise her with their erratic behavior. She pushed herself up from the bed, slipped her feet into her bunny slippers and slouched into the living room. Her flat was tiny, even by London standards, but she liked it. It didn't offer a lot of space but it was cozy, and she had a neighbor who didn't mind taking care of Snuggles when she was away.

She checked the feline's bowl and saw that it was, indeed, empty. She picked up the bulky bag of kibble and sprinkled some in the bowl, filling it up to the brim. "Here you go, honey," she said, caressing the cat's snowy silky fur and watching her dig in enthusiastically. Just what she was going to do as soon as she managed to drag herself over to Em's place. But first she needed to get the rest of this dried-up muck out of her hair.

A hot shower later, she felt like a human being again, and as she shrugged into a T-shirt and pulled on a pair of jeans, she thought about last night, and the trouble they'd had with making this Noble Dingles understand he was no longer part of the world of the living. She understood why, of course. It's not much fun to discover that suddenly, without warning, you're dead, and all that you've worked so hard to accomplish, is now a thing of the past.

Dingles obviously had a hard time letting go, which was understandable. But he had no right harming the Livermores with his ludicrous antics.

But how could they make him stop? First they needed to give him some kind of closure, by solving his murder. And for that, they needed Darian's help. He'd be able to figure out what had happened the night of Noble's murder. Maybe even solve the murder and catch the killer. Or perhaps the murder was already solved, and Noble simply wasn't aware of it. The dead were usually the last persons Scotland Yard thought to notify of an arrest.

Just then, her cell phone chimed and she saw that it was Jarrett. She checked the message, and smiled when she saw he was thinking the same thing she was. 'Let's ask Darian about Noble's killer,' the message read. That much was obvious. It was the next part that made her frown. 'Become Noble's allies—unleash the power of the scandal!' Um… what?

She quickly typed back, 'What are you talking about?'

Her phone rang and she picked up. "Hey, Harry," Jarrett said while she checked her hair in the hallway mirror. Her blond bob looked as shaggy as ever, but at least it wasn't a sticky, slimy mess anymore. Her golden eyes sparkled and her pixie face was finally clean again and devoid of ghost slime.

"What do you mean by becoming Noble's allies, Jarrett?"

"Just that," said Jarrett, his voice chipper. He'd obviously shrugged off last night's incident. "We need to make him think we're on his side in this."

"You mean, against the Livermores?"

"Exactly. We have to make him feel that we're his allies, and that we're going to do whatever it takes to get the Livermores out of his house."

She still didn't get it. "By unleashing the 'power of the scandal?'"

"Of course! If Noble wants a scandal, let's give him one! We'll tell him we're willing to nail Nathan Livermore to the wall of public shame. That whatever dirt he's got on the man, we're prepared to go public with it. That'll make him feel we're firmly in his camp and he'll slowly learn to trust us."

Horrified, Harry said, "But… we're working for the Livermores, Jarrett. *They* are our clients, not Noble Dingles. We can't expose their secrets."

"Yes, we can, as long as they don't know we're the ones doing the exposing."

She shook her head, a frown now etched on her brow. "But how…"

"Every tabloid has a hotline, Harry. And they promise absolute anonymity. Trust me, I've called them countless times. I know the drill."

"You have?" she asked, greatly surprised.

"Of course. Where do you think the tabloids get their information?"

"Um… well-meaning citizens?"

"Well-meaning citizens are sound asleep when the shit hits the fan, darling. No, Socialite A hates Socialite B's guts, so every chance they get to get them into trouble, they jump at the chance. And of course Socialite B returns the favor at the earliest possible convenience. It's all a game, Harry, and a fun one at that. So let's put Nate Livermore on the spot, shall we? Stir up a shitstorm of epic proportions. That will put us on Noble's dance card."

"I don't know," she said dubiously.

"What don't you know? It's a brilliant scheme!"

"It seems like an extremely circuitous way of gaining a ghost's trust."

"Trust me, this is going to be great," he gushed. "Nate Livermore won't know what hit him!"

"That's what bothers me. Nate Livermore is our client. Don't you think we should protect him from scandal, not create one?"

"No, I don't," he said decidedly.

"This scandal might destroy him."

"No, it won't. Nate needs this, Harry. He needs this badly. A man who wants to become Britain's Prime Minister needs to toughen up. This is what's going to put hair on his chest. It'll be the making of him, I promise you. It wouldn't surprise me if he thanks us on his bare knees once this is all over."

Somehow Harry doubted this.

*a*s usual, Harry covered the short distance between her apartment and Em's on her sturdy red bike. It wasn't that she couldn't afford a car, but she was so used to traversing the city on her beloved two-wheeler and so fond of the ease and practicality of getting everywhere a lot quicker than by car that the thought simply didn't cross her mind. Besides, owning a car would only exacerbate the smog issue that plagued the capital, and she didn't want that on her conscience. That, and she could use the exercise, of course. When you spend your days trying to reason with ghosts and chasing after them, it's important to stay in shape, and bicycling meant she didn't have to shell out for a gym subscription.

Even though money wasn't really an object these days, frugality was second nature to her. Her parents had died in a terrible car crash when she was in college, and so from a relatively young age she'd been forced to fend for herself and live well below her means. It was a hard habit to kick.

"Buckley," she now called out as she peddled along, slipping through the congestion with agility and grace. "What do you think about this mess?"

Sir Geoffrey Buckley was her former employer at the antique store that had carried his name. After he was murdered, she and Jarrett had worked together with Darian to find the culprit, and when they had, Buckley had decided not to join his dead brethren and sisters in the hereafter but to stick around, and effectively become Harry's guardian angel.

What's more, he'd left her his store and a small capital, and when the store had proved insolvent without his presence, had allowed her to sell it, which was the main reason that, for the first time in her life, she was now able to stare the future in the face with crispy banknotes lining her pockets.

Buckley usually hung around Harry's apartment, though lately he'd been hitting the town, doing a little sightseeing, and could often be found at the racetrack, where he slipped unsuspecting gambling paterfamilias a hot tip straight from the horse's mouth—literally, as horses apparently could see ghosts, and even chat with them, keeping him up to date on their form. If only he'd had this ability in life, he lamented, he'd have cleaned up.

In other words, he wasn't merely Harry's guardian angel, but fashioned himself some kind of Santa Claus these days, which, with his gray hair, kind face and eternal smile, was a job he seemed born for. And died, obviously.

He was now floating next to her, even as she picked up the pace to beat an orange light, and settled on her luggage carrier, looking a little pensive. His expressive face was puckered up into a frown, and he seemed as baffled by this Noble Dingles case as Harry and Jarrett were, apparently.

"The thing you need to keep in mind," he told her, raising his voice above the noise of hooting cars and gunning engines, "is that Noble Dingles blames the Livermores for his death."

"That's just dumb. They didn't kill him," she yelled.

"Well, they're the only ones he can see. In his mind they caused this sudden and shocking change in his life and he would like to see them go, hoping that will restore his life to normal."

"But he has to see that they've got nothing to do with his death."

"He should, but he doesn't. Since he doesn't know who killed him, and doesn't even begin to know how to find out, he simply blames everything on the Livermores, the people who've taken over his house and his life. You can understand that, can't you, Harry? Imagine if it was you who was suddenly murdered. Before you know what happens, suddenly a bunch of strangers invade your nice house, and you're forced to stick around and watch them throw out all your furniture, repaint your walls in a pukish green and generally behave like an invading army having no respect for the locals. If you were in his shoes, you'd want the Livermores gone, wouldn't you?"

"I guess I would," she admitted, never having looked at it from this perspective. That's why she liked that Buckley was part of the team: he gave them the ghost's perspective on things, a perspective she and Jarrett obviously lacked, because they weren't dead.

"Well, then you can see how Noble feels he's to be pitied rather than censured. That he's the victim here, and not the culprit."

"Do you have any idea who killed him?"

"As far as I can see whoever is responsible was connected to his job."

"His job? He was a simple civil servant, not an MI5 agent or something."

"He was a civil servant working for the Ministry of Defense, and as such had access to certain state secrets I should think. Perhaps you should take a closer look at his past, Harry. I'm sure you'll find this wasn't a mere home jacking or a robbery gone wrong. His death served a purpose."

"Thanks. And what about the theft of the Pink Eulalie? Any ideas who's behind that?"

She knew that Buckley used to be a well-known high-end fence, well-renowned for his ability to handle stolen antiquities and other items of value. If anyone knew who was behind the theft of the Pink Eulalie, it was him.

"I've been out of the loop for some time now, as you can well imagine."

Yes, being dead more or less took you out of that loop, she thought. Still. "Do you think Master Edwards could be involved?" she asked now, referring to the East End crime boss who had been one of Buckley's clients when he was still alive and well and rubbing elbows with the London underworld.

"No, I don't think Edwards is involved," he said. "These are not master thieves, Harry. It's my best guess they're glorified shoplifters who got lucky."

"They didn't plan to take the Eulalie?" she asked, making a sharp left and crossing paths with a taxicab, whose driver now honked furiously. She gave him a jovial wave, and ventured into an alley, a shortcut to Em's place.

"I don't think so. I have a feeling they're a bunch of rank amateurs."

"So Chuck and Elvis got lucky," she said.

There was a commotion, and when she turned to look, she saw that Buckley had fallen off the bike. He climbed back on. "What did you say?"

"Chuck and Elvis got lucky?"

"When I was still buying and selling antiques, I had dealings with a pair of idiot crooks who went by the name of Chuck and Elvis."

She turned to look at him in surprise, and barely missed a metal garbage bin. "I thought he was simply joking."

"Who?"

"Noble. He said he'd given Chuck and Elvis the combination of the safe. I figured he'd made those names up."

Buckley snapped his fingers. "Elvis Presley and Chuck Berry. Those were the guys. And there was a third one, a little smarter than the others. He was the one in charge. Fats Domino! That's it. You don't forget names like that."

"No, I can imagine you don't," she agreed.

"If they're the ones who robbed the Livermore place you can relax, Harry. They're not the sharpest tools in the criminal shed. In fact they're probably the dullest. It shouldn't be too hard to catch them, and the Eulalie."

"Thanks, Buckley," she said. One mystery was solved already. Now if only they could figure out who'd murdered that poor Noble Dingles, they could finally start figuring out how to shift him from the Livermore place.

CHAPTER 11

She'd arrived at Em's place and tied her bike to the wrought-iron fence that covered the basement window. She'd already had so many bikes stolen that she didn't take any chances. Then she hurried inside, Buckley preceding her by floating through the front door to the apartment complex. That was one advantage ghosts had over the living: they never had to ring the bell.

Five minutes later, she stepped into Em's apartment, her hostess looking a little under the weather. Emmanuella Sheetenhelm was a remarkably beautiful woman in her late fifties, who looked like a retired fashion model. She had a keen sense of style, both in her personal appearance and her apartment, which was a haven for any art aficionado. She always sported the latest artwork on prime display, and Buckley loved to come here, simply to bask in Darian's mother's exquisite taste.

Today she looked a little peaky, though. Her platinum hair hung listlessly around her high-cheeked face, her nose was red and when she spoke it was in husky, nasal tones. And when Harry asked if she was feeling all right, she said, "I think I caught a bug, darling." And then proceeded to sneeze heartily.

"Bless you," said Harry and Buckley simultaneously.

"Maybe we should do this some other time?" Harry suggested as she followed Em through the living room and out onto the spacious balcony, where a veritable green haven had sprung up under Em's loving guidance. A big ginger cat mewled plaintively at her feet, and proceeded to smell her trouser leg, probably detecting Snuggles's scent. She picked him up and said, "Hello there, Mr. Morris. You're not feeling so perky, are you?"

"Mr. Morris never gets a bug," sniffled Em. "And no, we shouldn't do this some other time. It's just a cold, darling. It will pass. Sit down. You, too, Buckley."

She gestured at the metal table which was set for breakfast, and Harry took a seat, gazing out across the back gardens of the neighboring houses. Even though it wasn't sunny out, and not very warm either, it was still warm enough to have breakfast out on the balcony, something Em was fond of.

Buckley, floating an inch above the chair, had his own plate and cup, though that was just for show, as he had left taking nourishment behind when he died. He still liked to preserve the niceties of having breakfast like a regular person, and went through the motions without uttering a protest.

"Darian is on his way," Em said as she poured tea into the cups.

"Great. We can tell him all about what we discovered," Harry said.

"Yes, what is all this I'm hearing about the Livermores?" asked Em, who was as keen to hear a bit of gossip as the next person, or perhaps even keener.

Harry took a bit of toast and started buttering it. "Well,

Jarrett and I got called in to deal with a haunting—a poltergeist," she explained between two nibbles. "And it turned out the place had just been robbed and the ghost we were sent to chase away was helping the burglars to get their hands on the contents of the safe."

"That's not very nice," said Em, with a disapproving glance at Buckley, as if, by being a ghost, he was responsible for the bad behavior of all ghosts.

"I don't know this ghost," said Buckley a little defensively.

"I'm not blaming you, Buckley," said Em, though she obviously was.

Just then, Darian walked out onto the balcony, and joined them. He was looking a little haggard, with dark circles under his eyes, as if he hadn't slept much, but otherwise appeared as big and imposing as usual. He was a hulking man, with shoulders and a chest that stretched any shirt he wore, and wouldn't have looked out of place in a David Gandy underwear commercial.

His dark hair was mussed, which was unusual for him, and when he bent over Harry to give her a brief peck on the lips, she caught a whiff of his aftershave, her new favorite scent in the world. He lingered for a moment, and said, "You smell... funny."

She rolled her eyes. "Must be the slime. How many times do I have to take a shower to get that smell out of my hair?! It's just terrible!"

"Slime?" he asked, taking a seat next to Buckley.

"Jarrett and I were slimed last night, by that Dingles ghost."

He grinned at this. "Great experience, huh?"

She nodded. "I guess it's something every ghost hunter has to go through at least once." Darian himself had been slimed not so long ago, in this very apartment, and it had left an indelible impression on him, especially since it was his first encounter with a ghost. Before, he'd been a ghost skeptic, but after that experience he'd joined the camp of the believers.

"Hey, Buckley," he said, greeting the old ghost. "Hi, Mum."

"Darian," said Buckley in acknowledgment. He'd already drifted a few more inches above his chair. The antiquarian had a hard time staying put.

"I've got a hot tip for you, honey," said Harry now, gesturing at Buckley with her head while she took a bite out of her toast. "Buckley knows the guys who burgled the Livermore house last night, don't you, Buckley?"

"Oh?" asked Darian, giving Buckley an expectant look.

"Their names are Elvis Presley, Chuck Berry and Fats Domino, with Domino working mostly behind the scenes. He's the mastermind, if you can call it that," he explained. "I'm sure that if you go after them right now, you'll find the loot, as they don't start to shift it until a week after the job, when things have started to settle down. At least that's how they used to operate."

"Thanks," Darian said. "You're right. We did find the loot."

Harry raised her brows. "You... caught them? Already?"

"We did," said Darian, raking his fingers through his hair. "One of the neighbors happens to be a light sleeper, and saw the van pull up at the house. He was suspicious, as the Livermores told him they were at some function, so he wrote down the license plate number. We found Chuck, Elvis and Fats in some dingy garage in Soho, where they were divvying up the loot."

"Hey, that's great news!" said Harry, proud of her sleuthing boyfriend.

"It is," Darian agreed. "The only thing missing from the scene?"

Her face fell. "Not the Pink Eulalie?"

He nodded. "When we asked, they said they'd never even

heard of the Pink Eulalie, which is impossible, of course, especially in their line of work."

"You should lean on them hard, Darian," said Em with lips pursed in disapproval. As a homeowner herself, she had very little patience with the burgling breed. Her apartment was littered with valuables, and if anyone dared violate the sanctity of her home, she'd fight them tooth and claw.

"I'm interrogating them this morning," Darian said, checking his watch.

"Don't you think you should get some sleep first?" asked Harry. "You look exhausted, honey."

He nodded, rubbing his eyes. "Didn't get much sleep last night, as you can imagine. But as long as we don't have that rock, we need to keep moving. For all we know it might be halfway to Antwerp by now, and then it's gone."

"Why Antwerp?" asked Harry, and the others all looked at her as if she'd just flubbed a question on QI, the BBC version of Jeopardy.

"Antwerp is the diamond capital of the world, hon," said Buckley with a smile. "If you want to get rid of a stolen diamond, that's the place to go."

"Oh," she said, nodding. "Right. Of course."

Buckley turned to Darian. "I don't think they'll have shipped it to Antwerp. I'm sure they happened upon the Eulalie quite by accident, which would mean they didn't have a plan in place for what to do with it."

"Do you think so?" the Scotland Yard inspector asked hopefully.

"Yes, I do. These are petty thieves, Darian. Like I told Harry, they're barely a cut above common shoplifters. They wouldn't know what to do with this ring. Nor would they have the contacts to shift it safely and swiftly."

"Which doesn't explain why we didn't find it amongst the

loot," he said pensively. He took a slow sip of the strong coffee his mother had brewed up.

"What's all this talk about the end of the monarchy?" asked Harry.

He practically spewed out his coffee. "Um, what?"

"Well, when I came into Nathan Livermore's study last night, you were discussing something about the end of the monarchy. Something that could cause quite a bit of embarrassment to the Queen? Was something stolen from that safe apart from the Pink Eulalie?" She was coloring a little pink herself now, for Darian was eyeing her with barely concealed exasperation.

"I can't discuss that, Harry, I'm sorry," he was quick to respond.

"So something else *was* stolen," she said, nodding. "Jarrett was right. Some documents belonging to Dame Victoria Smelt, perhaps? Her last will and testament, maybe? Stipulating that Nathan Livermore should be the next Prime Minister of the United Kingdom? Am I getting warm?"

Darian's jaw had dropped, and he now hitched it up. "How do you…" He closed his eyes, then continued, tersely, "Like I said, I can't discuss the specifics of the case with anyone, not even you, Harry."

"I just hope you find this will, Darian," she said with a worried frown. "If these three poops reveal the contents of Victoria Smelt's decree, it might spell trouble with a capital T. For Queen and country, not to mention Nathan."

"No need to speculate, Harry," said Darian. "My lips are sealed."

"You can discuss it with me, can't you, darling?" asked Em now. "Is it true what Harry is saying? Are they going to cause trouble for the Queen?"

"I. Cannot. Discuss. It," said Darian between gritted teeth.

"But I'm your mother, darling," Em pointed out. "I fed you, I bathed you, I gave you the milk from my—"

"Mother! I can't discuss any of this with anyone!"

Em rolled her eyes expressively, and then sneezed again. "If you can't even tell your own mother what's going on... You disappoint me, Darian."

At this, Darian rose to his feet. "I really have to go," he said. "I've got three poops, as you called them, to interrogate, one Pink Eulalie to retrieve and... stuff-that-can't-be-named to locate."

"Knock 'em dead, honey," said Harry.

"Yes, knock 'em dead," Em chimed in, and she meant it, too.

After Darian had left, Harry remembered Jarrett's plan to get the information about the contents of that safe from Noble and then leak it to the press. Perhaps she should have told Darian? But then she decided against it. If he wasn't sharing information, she wasn't sharing it either. Quid pro quo, as Hannibal Lecter would have said. Somehow, she felt he should trust her more. She was his girlfriend, after all. If he couldn't confide in her, who could he confide in? She looked up when she noticed Em giving her a keen stare.

"What?" she asked. "Do I have something on my face?"

"I think you should try to figure out what's going on, darling."

"Well, you heard him. He won't tell me."

"Oh, he will," said Em with a smug smile.

"But how? It's not as if I can drag it out of him."

"It's a little thing called pillow talk, darling. You should try it sometime. When Broderick had secrets to spill, but found himself unable to, I always managed to get him to spill them anyway." She gave Harry a cheeky wink.

CHAPTER 12

*A*s Darian strode into the New Scotland Yard headquarters, his phone beeped. When he took it out and checked the display he saw that Harry had sent him a message. He read it with a frown. 'Forgot to ask: could you check if Noble's murder was ever solved? Noble Dingles=poltergeist. XXX H.'

He smiled as he tucked his phone away. After having been a bachelor for the last fifteen years, he was taking things slowly, though he had the distinct impression that in Harry McCabre he'd found the woman he was prepared to share the rest of his life with. He simply hadn't told her yet. From the moment they met, he'd been pretty much bowled over by her charm, intelligence and quirky beauty. Now he couldn't imagine life without her.

True, they hadn't discussed moving in together, but that was only a matter of time. Soon, now, he would ask her to take things to the next level, and already he was starting to nail down the details. His mother, for one, kept urging him to get a move on, and to strike while the iron was hot.

"You're not getting any younger, Darian, darling," she

liked to say, making him feel older than Methuselah, even though he was only thirty-five. But she was probably right. A woman like Harry wouldn't wait around forever. If he didn't pop the question soon, she might go looking elsewhere.

He frowned as he set foot inside his office and draped his coat over the coat rack behind the door. He wondered who this Noble Dingles was. After a few quick checks, he discovered he was the guy who lived in the Livermore place before Nate and his family moved in. He'd died in what looked like a burglary gone terribly wrong, even though nothing was stolen, and the murder never solved. And as he looked deeper into the case file, something else caught his attention. Something very curious indeed.

Noble Dingles had worked for the Ministry of Defense, and his immediate superior had been... Nathan Livermore. Now how about that for a coincidence? He leaned back as his eyes scanned the file. Nothing else jumped out at him, so he finally closed it, and dragged his mind back to the Pink Eulalie case, or, as it was now known to him, the Victoria Smelt case.

They needed to get their hands on that will, before its contents were leaked to the outside world and they had a bloody scandal on their hands. He didn't care about the Pink Eulalie, though they needed to get that back, too, of course. He'd staked his reputation on its retrieval.

Ten minutes later he was seated across from Fats Domino, regarding the swarthy man sternly. In spite of the marked chill in the air-conditioned room, Domino was sweating profusely, which was a good sign.

"Mr. Domino," he said, opening proceedings. "There's only one thing I want to hear from you, and that's the location of the contents of the Livermore safe. Where is the Pink Eulalie? And where are the documents?"

Domino shrugged. "I have no idea what you're talking about, inspector."

"I think you do."

"All I can say is that my associates happened to happen upon a bunch of junk dumped on the sidewalk and were so kind to put it in their van so they could dispose of it in their local container park. If only all citizens were so mindful of keeping our streets clean and ridding it of unwanted junk, London would be a nicer, cleaner place, wouldn't you say?" He produced a smile.

Darian narrowed his eyes. "So why didn't you dispose of it? Why was it still lying around your so-called garage when we busted you?"

Domino lifted his shoulders. "The container park opens at ten, inspector."

"I think you're lying, Domino."

"That's your prerogative, inspector. If the public services worked around the clock, the same way hard-working citizens like myself and my associates do, we would have disposed of the loot—I mean the stuff, sooner."

"Where did they find... the stuff?"

"Just lying around," he said, making a display of studying his fingernails. "They said to themselves, 'What do we have here? What are this flatscreen TV, these iPads, iPods, laptops and that other junk doing lying around?' So they decided to do the right thing and clean it up. Another job well done. I call it a prime example of civic duty, inspector. Wouldn't you agree?"

"No, I wouldn't," he said forcefully. "Don't think for one minute that I buy that story, Domino. Your rap sheet and that of your two cronies—"

"I prefer the term associate, if you don't mind, inspector."

"Yes, I do mind." He tapped the man's file. "You've got a

rap sheet a mile long, Domino. So don't tell me you're a model citizen!"

"That's all in the past, inspector. I've got a kid to take care of now. A responsibility. I'm reformed."

Domino did have a kid, and from the information Darian had gotten at the hospital, she was pretty sick, too. Terminally, actually, which made him feel for the guy, but not enough to let him off the hook that easily.

"So Chuck and Elvis just so happened to pass by the Livermore house in the middle of the night, and they just so happened to find a flatscreen, a couple of laptops, a stereo…"

"And a few iPads and iPods and iPhones and a couple of paintings. It's a sign of the times, inspector. Consumerism is what it is. People keep buying the latest gadget and don't even value what they have. They simply throw it out. Lucky my guys happened to pass by and are so committed to recycling as much as they can. Our planet is dying, inspector."

"Is that so?"

"Oh, yes. And we all have to chip in to save her for future generations." He gave him a sad look. "For our children and our children's children."

"So you were simply doing us all a favor, huh?"

"That's right, sir."

"Saving the planet one flatscreen TV at a time."

He gave him a look of abject modesty. "I do what I can, sir."

"And your flunkies didn't happen to find a very nice, expensive diamond ring lying amongst the rubble? Or a pile of very private documents?"

"Oh, no, sir," said Domino, shaking his head. "Are they missing a ring?"

He tapped the table with his index finger. "You know as well as I do that they're missing a ring, Domino. A fifty million pound ring. Where is it?"

"I swear to you, inspector…"

"Enough already! Just tell me where it is!"

Domino's face cleared. "You know what must have happened? Another crew must have passed by and picked up the ring. They didn't even bother with the flatscreen TV and the other stuff, leaving that for my men to find."

Darian shook his head. This guy was simply too much. "Yeah, I'm sure that's what happened," he growled.

Just then, Constable Tilda Fret stuck her head in. "Inspector? A word?"

He gave Domino what he hoped was a penetrating and threatening glance, but the man simply smiled at him with a look of such innocence anyone who hadn't looked at his file would have thought he was an angel.

He closed the door behind him. "What is it, Tilda?" he asked, expelling a weary sigh. He needed more coffee if he was going to survive this day.

She shook her head. "We didn't find a thing, sir. We checked the garage, Domino's house, and the dumps where Elvis Presley and Chuck Berry live, and… nothing. Not a sign of the Eulalie or the documents."

"Oh, God," he said, pressing the palms of his hands against his temples.

"Are you all right, sir?" Tilda asked solicitously. She was a motherly, heavy-set woman with hair the color of the double-decker buses that were so prevalent in London and popular with the tourists. "Need an aspirin?"

"No, I'm fine," he said. "Where can they have put it?"

"They didn't have much time," she mused. "We barged in while they were still deciding what to do with the loot."

"So wherever it is, it can't be far. Send some uniforms to search that garage again, Tilda. Top to bottom. Tell them to leave no stone unturned. The Pink Eulalie and the documents have to be there. They simply have to."

"Will do, sir," she said. Then she grinned. "I just got word about my promotion, sir."

"Oh?" he asked, innocently. "And? What's the verdict?"

Her grin widened. "Thank you, sir. I'm sure you put in a good word."

"Well, I did tell the brass that I couldn't imagine a finer inspector."

"Thanks, sir."

"Just call me Darian... *Inspector* Fret."

"It-it-it's a dream come true, Inspector Watley," she stammered, clearly in the grip of a powerful emotion now. For a moment, Darian feared she might hug him, but she finally managed to control herself with a powerful effort.

"Now show me that you've earned that promotion and find me that Pink Eulalie, Inspector Fret. And, more importantly," he added, fixing her with a pleading look, "get me the will of that damned Victoria Smelt!"

CHAPTER 13

*T*here's something to be said for having breakfast out on the balcony of one's luxury suite, with a nice overview of the bustling capital. And for drinking hot coffee on an empty stomach. Doctors would probably disagree, but as Jarrett enjoyed his morning cuppa, reading his morning newspaper and enjoying buttered toast with marmalade, he thought doctors were overrated, especially when dealing with a medical anomaly like him.

He simply happened to be blessed with a stomach lined with Kevlar, and strong coffee had never bothered him. Quite the contrary. It gave him the impetus and the energy to start his day. For a man who was richer than most men in the country, he could probably have started his day by drinking tea soaked with tiny flecks of gold, but, even though he was an Englishman through and through, for some reason he didn't like tea. Sacrilege, of course, but there you had it.

When a loud harrumph sounded in his ear, he looked up from his perusal of the latest scandal that rocked Hollywood, and discovered that his father had joined him.

"Oh, father," he said. "I didn't hear you come in."

He folded his newspaper while his old man took a seat. He habitually joined him for breakfast, still harboring the faint hope that one day he'd find his son peppering him with questions about the business empire that the Zephyr-Thorntons had built, and ready to step into his father's insoles.

"So what have you been up to?" asked Jarrett Sr. He was a large, red-faced man with a drooping mustache and dentures to rival any Hollywood leading man. He now lowered a kippered herring into the abyss while waiting for his son's response. Unlike Jarrett Jr., Jarrett Sr. possessed a gloomy disposition, a consequence, no doubt, of being responsible for the livelihood of thousands of employees. It was only one of the reasons Jarrett Jr. had always refused to take over at the helm of the Zephyr-Thornton empire.

"Oh, this and that," he said vaguely as he watched his old man chomping down on the kippered herring and then adding another one to keep the first one company.

"What is it that you do all day?" asked his father, one of his favorite questions. "Tap-dancing?" he snorted loudly at his own suggestion. "Or collecting comic books? Or training to be a Formula One driver? What?"

"I did the Formula One thing, and it proved to be an absolute borefest. Driving round and round the track like a hamster on a wheel. Not for me," he confessed. "No, I've left all that silly folly behind me."

"Oh?" asked his father, greatly surprised. "So what do you do now? Your mother wants to know," he added, clearly hoping this would induce his offspring to open up about what was going on in his life.

"I told you already," said Jarrett, taking a dainty sip of coffee. "I'm into ghost hunting these days. Chasing them away from the homes they haunt, placating them with promises of a bright future in the hereafter, and generally making the ectoplasmic bunch pay attention and behave."

His father's eyes had widened at this. "But-but-but I thought you were joking when you told me about these Wraith Wranglers!"

"Well, I wasn't."

"But that's simply ludicrous! A load of poppycock! Sheer codswallop!"

"I can assure you that it's not," he said with a measured smile. "Ghosts exist, father, and they need a firm hand to make sure they don't misbehave."

"It's *you* who needs a firm hand," muttered his father.

"Be that as it may," he said, buttering his toast with his pinky finger sticking up just so, "this new hobby of mine is suiting me just fine. And I don't mind telling you that I'm becoming quite good at it, too."

"You can't be serious, Jarrett," grumbled his father, greatly dismayed.

"Oh, but I am. Dead serious, if you don't mind the pun."

"I don't get it."

"I thought you wouldn't. Dead serious, because I deal with the dead."

"I don't get why you have to throw your life away on this nonsense!"

"Well, it's my life, as Talk Talk used to say."

"I read the advertisement. Wraith Wranglers. Harry McCabre," his father sputtered, now so undone his plate remained untouched.

"Yes, a very agreeable young woman, and a great friend."

His father looked up at this. "A woman? This, um, this Harry person, she's a, I mean to say, she's a, well, a woman?"

"I did tell you about her, father," he said a little reproachfully.

Harry had been instrumental in saving Jarrett's mother's life, but his father had obviously forgotten about the role she'd played.

"So, um…" His father hesitated, fiddling with his herring. "You and this Harry, you get along great, eh? A wonderful friendship is blossoming and… something more, perhaps?" A hopeful smile was now spreading across his ruddy features. Or it would perhaps be better to call it a wide grin.

"Merely business partners, father, and dear, dear friends. Nothing more."

His father's smile quickly evaporated. "Nothing more, eh?"

"Not a flicker. Not even a smidgen."

"Still firm on the whole, um, gay thing?"

"Exceedingly firm."

"Right."

Ever since he'd stepped out of that particular closet, his father had harbored a hope against hope that this was merely a phase. A whimsical folly. Like leg warmers. Or Rubik's cubes. It wasn't a fad, though, and he'd had to speak to his father about this. Not that the man ever lost hope that one day his son would introduce a nice young lady of respectable lineage and announce his betrothal. It wasn't so much Jarrett's marital happiness he was concerned about, of course, but the production of an heir to the Zephyr-Thornton throne. One who would eventually inherit the vast empire the Zephyr-Thorntons had built. The fact that so far there were no heirs on the horizon obviously gave his father heart palpitations, which was understandable.

"We're actually working on a very interesting case right now," he said, ignoring his father's muttered laments. "Nathan Livermore's house was burglarized last night, and his wife's Pink Eulalie stolen…" He paused for effect, and judging from his father's expression of shock and horror, he hadn't been mistaken in assuming the news would have quite an impact. "…and the Victoria Smelt will," he added after a dramatic pause.

"You don't say," said his father in a low voice. "Pink Eulalie *and* the will?"

"I'm just on my way to interview the ghost who helped steal those items."

His father's face fell again. "The ghost? But son, simply listen to yourself!"

"I do. Frequently," he assured his father.

"You're gibbering!"

"I can assure you that I'm not," he said sternly. "And if you would have been slimed the way I was slimed last night, you'd feel differently about the wispy breed. Ghosts are among us, father, and they're not to be trifled with."

His father sat back, despair written all over his features. Not only wasn't he ever going to have grandchildren to dandle on his knee, but his son had gone off the deep end. Soon he would have to visit him at the local loony bin.

Just then, Deshawn stepped onto the balcony, carrying a tray of freshly toasted toast. He offered one to Jarrett Sr. "Another piece of toast, sir?"

Jarrett Sr. shook his head forlornly. "No, Deshawn." He then looked up at the man. "Can't you talk some sense into this infernal son of mine? Now he says he sees dead people!"

Deshawn gave him a small smile. "That's quite all right, sir. I see them, too."

"Oh, dear God!" cried Jarrett Sr., clasping his ruddy head with his sausage fingers. "The world's gone mad! Mad, mad, mad, mad, mad!"

Jarrett locked eyes with Deshawn. There was compassion in Deshawn's gaze as he kindly placed a tender hand on Jarrett Sr.'s shoulder. "If it's any consolation, sir, I have some freshly brewed Earl Grey. With lemon."

With a supreme effort, Jarrett Sr. pulled himself together. You don't run a billion-pound company by giving in to despair, and soon that fabled stiff upper lip was back in full force, and he said, "Thank you, Deshawn. I'll have some." And as he watched the loyal servitor disappear into the suite, he said, "Maybe I should adopt Deshawn. I'm sure he'd give me grandchildren."

"I doubt it very much, father," said Jarrett, dumping a lump of sugar into his coffee. "Deshawn and I are, how shall I put it, batting for the same team."

A frown appeared on his father's broad brow. "You mean..."

"Yes, I do."

"You and Deshawn are..."

"Yes, we are."

"So you and he are..."

"No, we aren't!"

"Pity," said his father, his shoulders slumping. "You could have adopted. Like Elton and David."

Jarrett laughed what he hoped was a careless laugh. "I don't think so, father. Can you imagine me? With a child? Just the thought!"

"Of course," said his father somberly. "What was I thinking? You're still a child yourself." At these scathing words, he promptly got up, dabbing his face with a napkin. "I have to be off. Things to do, people to meet... money to make," he added with a stern look at his offspring.

"Enjoy, father," he said graciously.

Jarrett Sr. shook his head and walked away, grumbling strange oaths under his breath. When Deshawn came tripping out with a fresh pot of Earl Grey and lemon, he was surprised to find that two had become one. "Has your father left, sir?"

"Very observant of you, Deshawn," he said, Jarrett Sr.'s words still rankling. "He was disappointed at my refusal to procreate. Or even adopt."

"A bundle of joy, sir?" asked Deshawn.

"Yes," he said, dabbing at the corners of his mouth with a monogrammed napkin. He gave Deshawn a curious glance. "He feels you and I should tie the knot and adopt, Deshawn. Just like Elton and David."

Deshawn's eyebrow flickered for a moment, indicative of a powerful emotion animating his bosom. Then he was himself again. "Very well, sir."

"Indeed."

"Ludicrous, of course, sir."

"My thoughts, exactly."

There was a momentary silence, as the two men stared at each other. Deshawn was the first one to break it. "Will there be anything else, sir?"

"No, Deshawn. That will be all."

CHAPTER 14

*B*uckley was used to wandering around on his own. He was, after all, a ghost, and as such invisible to most people. As a consequence, even in public, he was all by himself most of the time, except when he met other ghosts.

Not that he minded. He'd always been a very social person. You don't run an antique store for many years as a hermit—part and parcel of being a shop owner is being capable of chatting amiably with your clientele, inducing them to trust you enough to buy an old rickety gateleg table for a small fortune.

But now, as he roamed around Fats Domino's crime den in Soho, he would have liked to be able to express his frustration to the police officers engaged in the same activity he was engaged in: subjecting the dingy den to a thorough search for that infernal Pink Eulalie and that blasted Smelt will.

He recognized Constable Tilda Fret, who was one of Darian Watley's trusty sidekicks, and then there were about a dozen other, eager beaver buttheads likewise looking busy while accomplishing nothing, just like him.

They were all eager to impress the brass by unearthing the big prize, but so far had nothing to show for their industriousness, not unlike Buckley himself. He, of course, was in the advantageous position that he could look inside certain objects without having to take them apart, and could even look beneath the floor and into walls, almost like a human TSA full-body scanner.

So far, the place had yielded nothing, apart from an awful lot of old junk that was possibly related to Mr. Domino's hobby of taking apart cars and sometimes even putting them back together again. As a self-proclaimed gearhead, Domino seemed almost recklessly indiscriminate about the objects he collected, ranging from a dozen old bicycles to the engine of a speedboat.

And then there were the rats, of course, both alive and dead, which seemed to infest every square inch of this place. But of a ring there was no sign. Of course, a ring is a tiny object, and in a place that would have had the producers of *Hoarders* salivating and tripping over themselves in their rush to sign Fats Domino up for a star turn on their show, it was like looking for the proverbial needle in a haystack. Though why anyone would drop a needle in a haystack was beyond Buckley. It seemed like reckless endangerment to the poor horses who had to eat the haystack.

At the end of his tether, he was wondering whether he wouldn't be able to induce one of the dead rats to talk to him, but it appeared they'd all moved on to that great old rat litter in the sky. He tried to imagine how the scene had played out: Chuck, Elvis and Fats, holding their post-mission debriefing, not unlike SEAL Team Six after taking out some high-value target in Yemen. Then, suddenly, the place was awash with anxious and trigger-happy coppers. Fats wouldn't have had a lot of options to hide the stone and the documents. He'd have had to be pretty quick about it, and Buckley's best guess was that he'd hidden it in some hole in the ground, just like Saddam Hussein that fateful night in some farmhouse. Buckley had searched every last hole in the ground, but of the Pink Eulalie or the will there was no sign.

They'd found the former Iraqi leader through his fondness for fish. Perhaps they needed to figure out what Fats Domino liked? He looked around. Cars, obviously. So... And he was just on the verge of a brainwave, when excited voices interrupted his thought process. They were coming from the other side of the small garage, where Domino had fashioned himself a small kitchen, a spiffy new coffeemaker—undoubtedly pinched from some coffee-loving homeowner—perched on a plastic folding table, a few tattered and well-thumbed copies of Top Gear and Auto Express scattered about.

He quickly moved over to see what was going on, and saw that two constables had discovered a magazine depicting some popular starlet in all her nude glory. Disgusted, he turned away, and saw that Tilda Fret, likewise, wasn't too well pleased with this inappropriate display of boyish enthusiasm. There was a whole stack of these nudie magazines, and his esteem for the fallen burglar-cum-amateur mechanic dropped a few more points. Finally he gave up. It was obvious that wherever the stone and the Smelt will were, they weren't here, not unless Fats Domino had outsmarted them all, and had pulled off the perfect crime: to make fifty million quid vanish into thin air.

CHAPTER 15

*A*s Harry and Jarrett sped toward the Livermore house, driven by Deshawn in Jarrett's black Rolls Royce Phantom, she received a message from Darian, letting her know that the murder of Noble Dingles was still unsolved, but that he'd unearthed one interesting factoid: the man's superior officer at the MOD had been none other than Nathan Livermore himself.

She looked over at Jarrett, who was idly humming a tune that may or may not have been that popular anthem *It's Raining Men*.

"Did you know that your friend Nate was Noble's boss at the ministry?"

Jarrett looked pained. "May I remind you that dear old Nate and I were never chummy? We may have been boys together, but we weren't friends."

"Well, he must have known Noble, if he worked for him." She mused for a moment. "Perhaps that's why Noble hates Nathan so much. If he was his boss, maybe he was one of those psychotic ones. You know the kind."

"I certainly do," said Jarrett, who'd never worked a day in

his life. "I can't imagine Nate being a great boss. The man has all the hallmarks of a human gargoyle, his aim in life probably to make the lives of his underlings miserable at every turn. Forbidding the display of picture frames of loved ones, prohibiting the taking of nourishment while seated at the desk and even outlawing water cooler talk, if they even have water coolers at the MOD."

They'd arrived at the house, and alighted from the car.

"I just had a visit from my father," Jarrett told her as they walked up to the front door.

"How is your father?" She'd never met the man, but had heard great things about him. As possibly the richest man in England, she imagined he was a force to be reckoned with, and she pictured him as a cross between Richard Branson and Tony Stark. Distinguished yet rebellious. Worldly yet exuding charm and charisma, not to mention that elusive *je-ne-sais-quoi*.

But Jarrett had told her his father would never go in for waterskiing with a naked girl perched on his shoulders. It simply wasn't his style, and besides, Pearl, Jarrett's mother, would never allow it.

"He wants me to marry Deshawn and adopt," Jarrett now lamented. "Can you imagine? Me! A father!"

She smiled at this, and darted a quick look at Deshawn, who'd parked the Rolls and was now joining them on the steps leading up to the front door.

"Well, I can," she said. "You and Deshawn would make a lovely couple."

"Oh, please," he scoffed. "It's not because we live together that we necessarily have to sleep together, Harry. Just the thought."

"Why not? He's a great guy, and I'm sure he'd make you very happy."

But Jarrett looked horrified. "Look, ours is a very complicated relationship, Harry. Master and servant and all that damned rot."

"Well, it's been done before," she pointed out. "Just look at Anastasia Steele and Christian Grey. They're into the whole BDSM thing, right?"

He stared at her. "I have no idea what you just said, but it sounds awful."

Harry rung the bell. They'd made an appointment with Nicolle, and she hoped she hadn't forgotten about them, what with all the commotion of last night. She gathered that by now the Livermores had moved in again, and were probably busy taking stock of the mess the burglars had left behind.

"And adopt," Jarrett said. "Can you imagine me with a child?"

"I think you'd make a fun father," said Harry with a grin. "Any child would be happy to have you as a father," she added when he made a face.

"I'm not Madonna, Harry, or even Elton John. I can't go around adopting babies. Babies, I'm sure, will simply cramp my style. What am I going to do with them when I decide, on the spur of the moment, to fly to Mars and populate the first human colony? Because that might just happen, trust me."

"Populating the first human colony on Mars can't be a spur of the moment thing, Jarrett," she told him sternly. "Because you can never come back to Earth. They did explain that very carefully, didn't they?"

He frowned. "Who did?"

"Well, the people you talked to. The Martian colony people."

"I didn't talk to anyone. Just a thought that popped into my head just now."

"Oh, right," she said, thinking how fortunate it was that Jarrett changed his mind so often. She didn't feel like losing the best partner she could imagine in her ghost hunting endeavor to the Martian colonization nonsense.

"It was simply an illustration of the fact that I would make a lousy dad."

"You could always take the kids with you," she said, just to egg him on a bit. "I'm sure they'll welcome your children with open arms on Mars."

"Yes, but will they have good schools? That's always the trouble with these colonies," he said.

The door swung open, and Harry decided to temporarily shelve the topic of Jarrett and Deshawn's future offspring. Nicolle Livermore stood before them, and she looked even more worried than she had last night.

"The police have just returned most of the stuff that was stolen," she announced as she led them inside.

"Oh, but that's great news," said Harry.

The lady of the house didn't seem to agree. "Everything except the contents of Nate's safe. So no Pink Eulalie and no personal documents."

"They haven't found your engagement ring yet?" Harry asked.

"Or the documents?" asked Jarrett.

Nicolle shook her head, and Harry understood why she was looking so glum. As long as those items weren't returned, things weren't looking good. What are a flatscreen TV and some daft paintings when a fifty-million-pound diamond ring is missing and the Queen's secrets are in danger of becoming tabloid fodder? It was a nightmare for the Livermores, Harry understood.

"I'm sure Darian—I mean Inspector Watley—will find the rest of the stolen items soon," she said now, displaying her confidence in Darian. She knew him to be an extremely capable and conscientious cop. A little too conscientious, perhaps, as he refused to share information with his girlfriend.

"I don't know what to do," said Nicolle, wringing her hands. She seemed to have lost ten pounds overnight, Harry thought, and her face was gaunt and pale, the bags under her eyes clearly visible. She suddenly felt a strong urge to reach out and give the woman a hug, but refrained from doing so.

Instead, she said, "We may have some more information on your poltergeist, Mrs. Livermore."

"Oh? What have you found out?" asked Nicolle, taking a seat on the sofa and inviting her guests to do the same.

Harry looked around, and saw that some of the paintings that had been stolen were back in their original places, while others were placed against the wall, waiting to receive the same treatment. Even the flatscreen TV was back.

"Well, his name is Noble Dingles," she said, "and he's an ex-collaborator of your husband's at the ministry, apparently."

Nicolle frowned at this. "The name doesn't ring a bell, I'm afraid."

"As an added coincidence, he used to own this house. And he doesn't like the fact that you came to live in it after he passed away. He was murdered, you see, and hasn't come to terms with the way he died so horribly."

"Oh, the poor man," said Nicolle, bringing a hand to her face in obvious consternation. "I can't imagine what a terrible ordeal it must be for him. First being murdered and then having his house overrun by a bunch of strangers."

"Well, not strangers, exactly," Harry pointed out. "Um, didn't your husband ever mention Mr. Dingles? He must have known him from the ministry, I would imagine. Unless he's not all that hands-on as a manager?"

"Oh, no, Nate is very hands-on. He cared deeply about the people who worked for him. Even invited them over for dinner if he felt that they were deserving of the treat. I can't tell you how many of his people I've met."

"He doesn't work at the ministry anymore?" she asked.

"No, Nate is a Member of Parliament now."

Just then, Pia appeared in the doorway, and stared at her mother with an annoyed look on her pretty face. "Mum. I can't find my iPad. Are you sure the police returned it?"

"Just look in the garage, honey. Perhaps it's still in one of the boxes."

She turned back to her guests. "The police have dropped everything off just now, so I haven't had time to go through all of it yet."

"So... Noble Dingles," said Harry. She now produced her smartphone and brought up Noble's picture. "Do you recognize him, Mrs. Livermore?"

Nicolle stared at the picture, and quickly shook her head. "No. No, I don't, I'm afraid." Then, much to Harry's surprise, she abruptly rose and said, in measured tones, "Now if you'll excuse me, I have a lot of things to deal with right now. I trust you know your way out?" And she promptly disappeared through the door, leaving the trio feeling a little bewildered.

"She knows Noble," Jarrett said. "I'm absolutely sure of it."

Harry nodded. "She recognized him, all right. But what does it mean?"

"It means that Nicolle hasn't been entirely honest with us," said Deshawn.

"Do you think she had Noble over for dinner?" asked Harry.

"She might have," Jarrett said. "Why don't we ask him?" And without waiting for a response, he pursed his lips. "Oh, Noble, where art thou?"

As if he'd been waiting in the wings, the ghost of Noble Dingles suddenly reared up from the floor, where apparently he'd been cooling his heels while they were having this conversation with Nicolle Livermore.

"I'm glad you're back," he said anxiously, then directed a curious look at Deshawn. "Who are you?"

"My name is Deshawn. Deshawn Little," Deshawn said in his velvet voice. "I'm Mr. Zephyr-Thornton's personal gentleman."

"And a very gentle man," added Harry for good measure.

"A working man, eh?" asked Noble. "I like you already, Deshawn."

"That's very gratifying, Mr. Dingles," said Deshawn with a nod.

"Look," said Noble, addressing Harry, "there's been a development."

"What development?" asked Harry, glad they weren't being slimed.

Noble grimaced. "I just saw the man who killed me."

"You did? Where?!" asked Jarrett.

"He was here just now. At the house."

"Who was it?" asked Harry urgently.

"One of the cops who returned the stolen stuff."

There was a stunned silence, as they processed this incredible bit of news.

"Are you sure that he was a cop?" asked Harry.

Noble nodded. "You don't forget the face of the man who killed you," he said. "It's forever engraved in my memory. He was here to return the loot."

Harry and Jarrett shared a worried glance. "We have to tell Darian," said Harry. "He must be told that one of the men working for him is a murderer."

"What's more, he knows Nathan Livermore," continued Noble. "At least that's the way I interpreted the short exchange between them."

"Nathan Livermore was your boss at the MOD, wasn't he?" asked Harry.

"Yes, he was. And a great boss, too. We all liked him tremendously."

"You liked him?" asked Jarrett, greatly surprised.

"Oh, yes. He was a real mensch, if you know what I mean. Always making sure that we were taken care of. Creating a very enjoyable working environment. In fact I think he was one of the best bosses I ever worked for."

"Then why do you want to scare him and his family away?" asked Harry.

He gave her a hard stare. "It's not because I liked him as a boss that I want him living in my house, Miss McCabre. He can get his own place."

"Just call me Harry," said Harry.

"I even had dinner with the Livermores once. Nathan used to have this 'Take a Worker Home For Dinner' thing and so I got to meet his family."

"So you did have dinner with the Livermores," said Jarrett.

"Yes, I did. Look, the Livermores are perfectly nice people," said Noble, "but I still don't want them living in my house. That is simply not done."

"An Englishman's home is his castle," intoned Deshawn, earning himself an appreciative smile from Noble. "And an Englishwoman, of course," he added in deference to Harry.

"Would you recognize the killer if I showed you a picture?" asked Harry.

"Of course. I would recognize him anywhere."

"I'll call Darian," said Harry. "We need to figure out who this guy is."

"And what his connection to the Livermores is," said Jarrett.

"Yes, I do find it curious how Nicolle Livermore vehemently denied ever having met Mr. Dingles," Deshawn said. "It seems suspicious, almost."

Harry moved over to the window, which looked out across the backyard, and took out her phone. The call went straight to voicemail, which told her Darian was probably still interrogating the burglars who'd robbed the Livermores. She left an urgent message. "Darian. Noble recognized one of the officers who came over to the Livermore house just now to return the stolen loot as the man who killed him. Please call me as soon as you get this."

When she turned back to the others, she saw that Nicolle Livermore was standing right behind her, looking none too happy. And as her gaze dropped to her hands, she saw she was holding a small gun, pointed at her heart.

"Please don't make any sudden movements, Miss McCabre," said Nicolle, her voice taking on a serious note. "Trust me, I won't hesitate to use this."

CHAPTER 16

*I*t is never pleasant to be invited into the home of a friend and end the visit tied up and gagged in the broom cupboard. Harry hadn't seen this coming, that much was certain, and she couldn't help experiencing a twinge of resentment toward the woman she'd taken such a liking to. Nicolle Livermore, she now saw, wasn't the hospitable future wife of the next Prime Minister of the United Kingdom, but a dangerous gun-wielding maniac who probably had more secrets to hide than MI5, FSB and the CIA combined.

"You won't get away with this," had been her last words before the woman shoved a scarf over her mouth and fastened it behind her head.

It had done much to halt the pleasant flow of conversation, especially since it was her own scarf, and one of her favorite ones at that. Deshawn and Jarrett had had to make do with scarves from Oxfam by the looks of them.

"We'll see about that," Nicolle had responded tensely as she inspected the ropes she'd used to tie Harry's hands and those of her associates.

Much to Harry's surprise, she'd proceeded to switch off

the lights, close the door, and had left them to their own devices, presumably to get in touch with her husband for instructions what to do with these Wraith Wranglers.

So they sat there, gathering dust, and Harry, like Nicolle Livermore, wondered what their next steps should be. Was this woman really a cold-blooded killer? Was she involved in the murder of Noble Dingles and if yes, what had been her motive? Why would she kill a harmless Ministry of Defense civil servant? Had he insulted her cooking the night he came to dinner? Had he made a pass at Nicolle's teenage daughter? Or were Nicolle and Nathan Livermore simply the new Fred and Rosemary West?

She hadn't the foggiest, but all the sympathy she'd ever felt for Nicolle and her plight had suddenly vanished like snow in the Sahara Desert.

She tried to push the scarf away with her tongue, but that didn't work, of course. Her tongue simply wasn't long enough, and she suddenly envied a frog, who'd have made short shrift of the scarf. She then shuffled over to what she knew was a wooden IKEA rack, and managed to drag the scarf down by hooking it behind a bolt and pulling. Finally, after twisting her neck in a yoga posture that would have made Gwyneth Paltrow proud, she managed. Gasping, she cried, "Jarrett! Deshawn! Are you all right?"

There were grunts of acknowledgment from both men, and she shuffled over in the direction they were sitting. She didn't have the advantage of sight, but when she bumped a body, she immediately reached out and started nuzzling what she knew was Deshawn, who'd been placed closest to her. She found the rag and took a firm grip with her teeth... and dragged it down.

"Oh, thank you, Harry," said Deshawn. "This isn't much fun."

"No, it's not," she grimly agreed. "What's gotten into Nicolle? Has she gone completely, stark raving bonkers?"

"Perhaps she was always mad," Deshawn offered a daring theory.

"She must have overheard me talking to Darian about Noble's killer. Which means she's—"

"Involved in the murder," Deshawn agreed. "It's the logical conclusion."

"So she knew Noble and had him killed. But why?"

"Your guess is as good as mine."

A loud muffled noise interrupted this easygoing exchange of ideas, and Harry remembered that Jarrett was still tied up. Deshawn did the honors, following Harry's successful formula, and soon Jarrett, too, was able to speak.

"Oh, whew!" cried Jarrett. "It isn't much fun being gagged!"

"No, it's not," Harry agreed.

"And with an Oxfam scarf, no less! I do hope they wash these things!"

"Are you all right, sir?" asked Deshawn.

"Well, as all right as one can be after being tied up like a sausage, silenced with an Oxfam scarf and unceremoniously dumped in a broom cupboard the size of Harry Potter's." He sniffed audibly. "I can smell the Dettol already."

It was a nice summary of the situation. "Now if we could get rid of these ropes," said Harry, tugging at them in vain. Whoever Nicolle Livermore really was, she definitely knew her knots, which indicated that at one point she'd been a Girl Guide. No matter how much she tugged, she couldn't get any wiggle room for her fingers to work the knots.

"This is the end," said Jarrett now, sounding uncharacteristically grave. "They're going to murder us and dump our bodies in a freshly dug grave in the backyard. I just know they will." He heaved a soft sob. "I want you to know, Harry, that I consider you the sister I never had. A dear, dear friend and the woman I'll never stop admiring for sheer pizzazz, panache and flair. It was an honor to know you, and I hope that once we're dead, we'll still get to hang out, only as ghosts this time. Don't be a stranger, Harry McCabre."

"Oh, Jarrett," said Harry, touched by these words.

"And Deshawn," said Jarrett, not wanting to waste time, for you never knew when the end was coming, "it's been an honor to know you. You were always more than a valet to me, and I consider you one of my best friends."

"I, too, consider you a friend, sir," said Deshawn huskily.

"I think in this, our final hour, you can suspend with the sir, Deshawn."

"Yes, sir. I mean, Jarrett."

"This isn't the end, boys," said Harry now. "We *will* get out of this, and Nicolle Livermore *will* be punished for her crimes. The Wraith Wranglers will rise again," she added, even though she had a hard time believing it herself.

For some reason, the gash in Noble's throat kept drifting before her mind's eye, and already she thought she could feel a similar slash being administered to her own throat. Ironic, she felt, that after spending so much time helping ghosts to move on, she would soon be a ghost herself. At least she'd have Jarrett and Deshawn to keep her company in the long, dark nights. She'd haunt Darian, she now decided, perhaps even move in.

Even though human-ghost relationships were a difficult proposition, they could make it work. Perhaps they could even get married, the ceremony presided over by a priest who could see ghosts. But would Darian still want her when she was dead? Perhaps he preferred a living, breathing woman?

And if she did move in with him, would she be able to get used to the terrible color scheme of his apartment? Only

Lord Voldemort could truly appreciate those black surfaces and that horrible chrome. And who was going to take care of Snuggles? Would Mrs. Peach be willing to take her in? And who would take over her apartment? Already she resented anyone who'd throw away her collection of little things and occupy her cozy nook.

She now understood how Noble had felt when the Livermores moved in.

"I just hope that whoever takes my apartment takes care of my plants."

"I thought you said we were going to survive this?!" cried Jarrett.

"Well, we are, of course, but it's still prudent to prepare for the worst."

"Oh, no! I'm not ready to die! There's still so much I want to do!"

"I thought *you* said you were a Wraith Wrangler forever?" asked Harry.

"I am! I mean, I was. But I also wanted to learn water badminton and wear those funny bathing caps. Be a BBC snooker commentator. Become the next Top Gear presenter. Join the Spice Girls on stage for their comeback tour and..." His voice dropped. "Join Madonna in Malawi and adopt twins."

Deshawn emitted an audible gasp. "You mean to say..."

"Yes, I do mean to say, Deshawn."

"Oh, sir—I mean, oh, Jarrett."

"Oh, Deshawn."

"What seems to be the trouble?" suddenly a grating voice interrupted.

Harry turned in the direction of the voice, but of course she couldn't see who it belonged to, as the lights were still turned off. But then she recognized it as Buckley's, and cried, "Buckley! Finally!"

"We've been captured, Buckley," said Jarrett. "By Nicolle Livermore."

"That's not very nice of her," said Buckley reprovingly.

"Oh, hello there," another voice piped up. "It's so cozy in here."

"Oh, hi," said Buckley. "You must be Noble Dingles, right?"

"That's me. And who are you?"

"Sir Geoffrey Buckley. I'm with Harry and Jarrett and Deshawn. Part of the team. I used to be an antique dealer until I was brutally murdered."

"Same here," said Noble. "Except I wasn't an antique dealer."

"Bludgeoned to death?" asked Buckley.

"No, throat slit."

"Oh, how was that?"

"Painful. How was being bludgeoned to death?"

"Not very pleasant," Buckley conceded.

"Still, not as unpleasant as being garroted I imagine. I was talking to Mrs. Beasley, who used to live across the street. She was garroted last spring. Said it was a most painful way to go. Wouldn't recommend it to anyone."

"I heard that about drowning," said Buckley. "Avoid it at all cost, Mr. Dingles. I was talking to a guy the other night, and he told me—"

"Could you suspend with the 'Nine Best Ways to Die' talk for the moment?" asked Jarrett, peeved. "And help us escape this broom cupboard?"

"Oh, of course," said Noble, suddenly a lot more accommodating. Perhaps he was starting to view his present company as all right, especially since they were now also being targeted by the Livermores.

"How are you on your knots?" asked Buckley.

"Oh, I'm sure I can manage," said Noble. "I learned to handle physical objects a week into my death."

"Hey, me too," said Buckley. "Once you get the hang of it, it's not all that hard. Only last week I actually managed to pop a sandwich into the toaster."

"Whatever for? You know you can't eat them, right?"

"Well, I was doing it as a favor to Harry. Harry's always in a hurry."

"Oi! Guys!" cried Jarrett. "Ropes?"

Within a few minutes, the three of them were finally free to use their hands again, and Harry switched on the light, then gave the door a tug.

"Locked," she concluded when it failed to yield to the pressure.

"Allow me," said Buckley, as he floated through the door. There was a resounding and very pleasant clicking sound and the door swung open.

"So easy to have a ghost on your team," said Jarrett appreciatively.

"It is indeed," concurred Deshawn, eyeing Jarrett a little awkwardly.

Jarrett fiddled with his Oxfam scarf. "Um, Deshawn…" He cleared his throat, dropped the Oxfam scarf as if it had cooties, and fiddled with his shirt. "Um, well, that is to say… I mean to say…"

"Boys, why don't you discuss this whole adoption thing later?" suggested Harry. "First we need to get out of this house, warn Darian that we were held at gunpoint by Nicolle Livermore, and tell him she's probably a killer."

"I knew Nathan should never have married a call girl," said Jarrett.

"Nicolle Livermore is a call girl?" asked Buckley, interested.

"Yes, she is. Her maiden name is Nicole Tart, which seems rather apt."

"And to think we used to say she was a Russian spy," said Noble now.

"A Russian spy?" asked Harry. "What made you think that?"

"Oh, it was just one of those rumors floating around the office. You know, office gossip. And of course there was the fact that I saw her walking out of the Russian embassy one day, a briefcase pressed under her arm." He laughed. "Gave the guys at the ministry something to talk about, that."

CHAPTER 17

*J*arrett stared at Noble, flabbergasted. This was all getting a bit thick, he felt. First Nicolle Livermore had been a lady of pleasure, then the wife of an important civil servant and a homemaker, and now she was a Russian spy and a vicious killer of Wraith Wranglers? He had the feeling they were coming over the plate a little too fast. On top of all that he'd just announced he was ready to follow in Madonna's footsteps and trot over to Malawi to fetch himself an orphan—if there were any left, of course—and start a family with Deshawn, effectively becoming the new Elton and David.

"A Russian spy?" he asked, just to make sure he'd heard this right.

"She could have been at the embassy to apply for a visa," said Noble.

"What do you say we get out of here first?" hissed Harry, darting anxious looks around the kitchen, obviously expecting the alleged Russian spy to come barging in, brandishing her peashooter, and her Oxfam scarves.

"You're right," he said. "We need to put as much distance

between ourselves and Nicolle as humanly possible." And since he knew the place pretty well, from the parties he'd attended here over the years, he quickly sped through the kitchen and started making his way to the door, which led into the backyard, where they could hop the fence and make their escape.

The others followed him, like ducklings waddling behind mother duck, and even Buckley and Noble were part of the conga line, even though they had nothing to fear from Nicolle, as they were dead already, and one of those immutable laws of being dead is that you can only die once.

And they would have made it, too, if Deshawn hadn't accidentally nudged a frying pan that was still on the stove, and allowed it to drop to the floor with a clattering noise that was loud enough to raise the dead, and certainly enough to draw the attention of Nicolle. Jarrett made a dash for the door, but even before he reached it, an icy voice halted his progress, and now that he came to think of it, there was a hint of Russian in Nicolle's delivery.

"Where do you think you're going?"

"Um, to get some fresh air?" he suggested.

He noticed she was clutching that gun in her hand again, aiming it loosely at his head, and he gave her his best smile in return. "You don't really plan to use that, do you, Nicolle? On an old friend like me?"

"You're no friend of mine, Jarrett," she said coldly.

"And here I thought we were chums," he said, shaking his head.

He saw she was frowning at their remarkably rope-free hands and scarf-free faces. "How did you get out of there?" she asked. "The door was locked."

"We have our ways," said Harry defiantly. "You killed Noble Dingles, didn't you?" she threw into the woman's face. "Sliced his throat!"

"I did no such thing."

"No, she didn't kill me," said Noble. "It was the cop. I told you guys."

"But she was involved," said Harry.

"Who are you talking to?" asked Nicolle, that frown still etched on her brow. She obviously wasn't afraid to get wrinkles, which just went to show you never really knew a person, for the old Nicolle had been just as obsessed with Botox and chemical exfoliants and microdermabrasion as her friends.

"Nobody," said Harry, then amended, "Or actually, somebody. I'm talking to the man you had killed. Noble Dingles."

Her frown deepened. "You're talking to the ghost of Noble Dingles?"

"Yes, I am."

"Well, tell him that if he doesn't clear out and leave my family in peace I'm going to kill his friends and turn them into ghosts also."

"Tell him yourself," said Harry. "He's right here."

Nicolle's eyes darted through the kitchen, but it was obvious she couldn't see Noble. She gestured with the gun. "Point him out to me. Now!"

"Over here," said Harry, gesturing at Noble, who hadn't moved.

"Tell her that if she kills my friends, I'm going to haunt her for the rest of her life, and I'll make her life so miserable she'll wish she was never born."

"He says that if you kill his friends—aw, Noble, that's so sweet of you."

"The enemy of my enemy is my friend," he declared solemnly.

"Well, anyway, he says he'll haunt you for as long as you live, and possibly even longer," Harry said, giving Nicolle the CliffsNotes version.

Nicolle shrugged. "I don't care. Now that I know it's only stupid Noble Dingles..." She gestured with the gun. "Now back in the cupboard, the lot of you. Move! Now!"

And to add emphasis to her words, she fired a single shot into the ceiling. From right above her, there was a loud yell. "Hey, Mum! I'm right here!"

"Oh, sorry, baby!" she yelled back. "Did I hit you?"

"No, but you killed my hairdryer!"

"Don't worry. I'll get you a new one!"

There was a pause, then Pia hollered, "You also killed my iPhone!"

"Nice try!" cried Nicolle, then gestured with the gun. "Why are you all still standing there? Didn't I tell you to get into the cupboard?! Move!"

Jarrett wondered how much Pia knew about her mother's homicidal tendencies. He held up his hands in a gesture of supplication. "You're not going to kill us in front of your daughter, are you? That would be cruel."

"Don't worry about my daughter, Jarrett. In you go, the lot of you."

But before she could say another word, suddenly the gun was slapped from her hand, and then she was lying flat on the floor, her legs having been kicked from under her and her body pressed down, for Noble and Buckley had decided to weigh in on the matter, taking a seat on the woman's back.

"Thank you, Buckley," said Jarrett

"And thank you, Noble!" Harry added.

"Get off of me, you moron!" cried Nicolle, offering proof that her refinement was but a layer of veneer covering a much darker core.

This time it was her turn to be trussed up and shoved unceremoniously into the broom cupboard. And as they stood conferring for a moment, wondering what their next course of action should be, suddenly Pia appeared, clutching her phone, and when she saw what was going on, and heard her mother's loud cries coming from the cupboard, she gasped in shock, and then was gone, racing away at a surprising rate of speed.

Ten minutes later, the cavalry arrived, in the form of Inspector Watley and his new partner Inspector Fret, and when Nicolle Livermore was carted off, handcuffed and defiant, and Harry and Jarrett and Deshawn had finished filling them in on the latest upheaval to rock the house of Livermore, it was obvious that the plot was thickening quicker than suet pudding.

As usual, Darian refused to share any information on what had transpired at the police station, and when finally they watched the panda car drive off with Nicole Livermore locked away in the trunk—or rather the backseat—Jarrett thought this was probably the weirdest case he'd ever been involved in. And since he was a Wraith Wrangler, that was saying something.

CHAPTER 18

"What's all this nonsense I keep hearing about Victoria?"

Mabel looked up from her notes. "Excuse me, ma'am?" she asked politely.

"Victoria. My cousin! That will she supposedly had drawn up keeps cropping up again and again. She's supposed to have promised Nathan Livermore the Prime Ministership! A load of poppycock, of course."

The Queen's secretary stared at her and blinked. Mabel Swainston was an owlish woman, whose overly large glasses managed to obscure a large part of her face. What there was of it that was visible to the human eye wasn't much to look at, which was perhaps the reason for the obfuscation. She had an oblong face tapering down to a pointy chin, and her hair appeared to have been placed on top of her head by a careless hand. The end result was a disconcerting jumble that turned heads. Not because of her stunning beauty but because people loved to play the 'What's Wrong With This Picture' game.

"Haven't you read the news, Mabel?" the Queen asked annoyedly.

They were seated in the sovereign's magnificently appointed study, where she held her daily meetings with her secretary. The Queen, in spite of her advanced age, was in fine fettle as usual. For the occasion she was clad in her favorite floral dress, her white hair tied back in a tight bun, and her feet shod in sensible white shoes of the kind often favored by nurses. She'd have preferred to potter about the palace in her comfy old housecoat, as she didn't have any official engagements today, but people would talk so she didn't.

She thoroughly disliked all this unfounded speculation about Nathan Livermore being earmarked as the next PM just because Cousin Victoria supposedly said so in her will, and found it hard to give credence to the rumor. Victoria had always been the more sensible one in the family, and would never have suggested something as preposterous as a cabinet appointment.

Even she, a veteran of British politics for more than sixty years, had absolutely no say in the matter whatsoever. There were elections to be held, negotiations to be conducted, and eventually a candidate selected, all without any input from the monarch. The notion that a member of the aristocracy would hold any sway was outrageous, and still the story kept being regurgitated with regular intervals in all the major papers, even the so-called serious ones. It was time to put a stop to this nonsense once and for all.

The matter revolved around the so-called Smelt will, a document that probably didn't even exist, as no one had ever laid eyes on it, except for Nathan Livermore himself, and even that wasn't a foregone conclusion. Personally she had always held the view that Nathan had simply spread the rumors about the Smelt will himself, as a means to further his career. Cunning strategist that he was, he had simply invented the whole story.

If the entire political class, and by extension the press and the population, thought he was being groomed for the top job, the powers that be might just grant him his wish and propel him into that position. It was simply a self-fulfilling prophecy, and nothing to do whatsoever with dear Cousin Victoria.

"We have to put a stop to this nonsense once and for all," she said determinedly. With the latest rumors swirling that the will had been stolen from the Livermore home, and the Pink Eulalie as well, media attention was mounting, leading to opinions being voiced that the royal family should be barred from interference in the electoral process. As if Victoria would have wished to interfere in anything. Simply the idea! If she'd known how her good name was being abused, she'd be sick to death, a sensible woman like her.

"Yes, ma'am," said Mabel obediently, as she made copious notes.

"Get in touch with our Scotland Yard liaison, and advise them to keep us fully informed. The moment the will and the ring are recovered, I want to know about it immediately. And express the wish that this matter should be resolved as soon as possible and with the utmost discretion."

"And what about the arrest, ma'am?" asked Mabel.

"What arrest? What are you talking about?" she asked as she smoothed her dress. It had a tendency to ride up at the hips, and at her age she didn't like to show more skin than was strictly necessary.

"The arrest of Nicolle Livermore. She's been taken into custody."

"Oh, dear," said the Queen, bringing a hand to her rosy cheeks. She rarely registered shock, having been through a long and eventful life, but she certainly did so now.

"She attacked a crew of the Wraith Wranglers who were at her home to chase away a ghost," supplied the secretary, eyes wide in excitement.

"Wraith Wranglers? You mean those people who claim to see ghosts?"

"Yes, ma'am," said Mabel, her face also flushed now. "They chase them away. There have been many reports that they're quite successful at it, too."

The Queen directed a censorious look at her secretary, and a rebuke was on the tip of her tongue. She didn't go in for all this newfangled nonsense. Wraith Wranglers, indeed. Simply misleading the public and demanding exorbitant fees, no doubt. This entire situation was getting out of hand. Nicolle Livermore probably hadn't agreed to their terms, and had tried to get rid of them like any sensible woman would. And now she was languishing in prison for it? This simply wouldn't do. She pursed her lips and a steely look came into her eyes, the look many a foreign dictator had learned to fear.

"I want it to be known to the Scotland Yard person in charge of the case that I vehemently protest this state of affairs. Arresting Nathan Livermore's wife indeed. They should have arrested these Wraith Wranglers instead."

"One of them is Jarrett Zephyr-Thornton, ma'am," said the secretary.

This gave her pause. "*The* Jarrett Zephyr-Thornton? The billionaire?"

"The son, ma'am. Not the father."

She nodded. "The wastrel, yes." She recalled how the boy's father had often lamented his son's descent into idleness. As one of England's most prominent businessmen, the boy's behavior was a disgrace not only to his father, but to the nation as a whole. Tabloid fodder in the days when he was the most outrageous party pooper ever to step out onto the

London nightclubbing scene, he'd recently calmed down somewhat, and had tried his hand at numerous ventures that had all led to nothing.

"He runs the Wraith Wranglers along with a former antiquarian."

The sovereign lifted her chin. "It doesn't surprise me that the boy would stoop so low," she said primly, her eyes betraying her disdain. "Well, it only strengthens me in my conviction that a great wrong was done today, Mabel. Nicole Livermore isn't the one who should have been placed under arrest, but rather this young imbecile and his wraith wrangling cohorts. Please convey my message that I want to see justice prevail, and this great wrong righted."

"Perhaps we should wait until we've been apprised of all the facts pertaining to the case, ma'am?" Mabel ventured. She was a prudent soul.

She waved a hand. "I think I've heard quite enough to make up my mind, Mabel. I want this matter resolved right speedily and, most of all, discreetly." She stared at Mabel with glittering eyes. "First and foremost, I want this matter of Victoria's will to be handled once and for all. As soon as the will has been retrieved I want its contents to be made public. Yes, you heard me."

"But, ma'am," said the secretary, gulping a little.

"There can be no mystery surrounding dear Victoria's last will and testament. As long as there is, rumors will continue to swirl, and I won't have it," the Queen said sternly. "Victoria would never have wanted her name used to further her grandnephew's political ambitions, I'm quite sure of it. Nathan should know better and we will put a stop to this at once."

"That means Nathan might never become the PM."

The Queen nodded curtly. "So be it. We live in a democracy, Mabel. The royal family doesn't play favorites and we don't go in for nepotism. We can't have the population thinking we're a bunch of nosy busybodies who stick our noses where they don't belong. Ere long they'll give serious thought of turning this country into a damn republic. A lot depends on this, Mabel."

"Of course, ma'am."

"And secondly, I want this Wraith Wranglers matter handled. I will have no such nonsense in my realm," she said, blithely contradicting her earlier statement the royal family didn't stick their noses where they didn't belong.

"What do you want me to say, ma'am?"

"I want the Wraith Wranglers arrested, and Nicolle Livermore exonerated, and that's my final word on the matter. See to it that it's done."

"Nicolle exonerated... Wraith Wranglers arrested..." Mabel muttered as she jotted all this down in her neat hand. Finally, she looked up, blowing a straying strand of hair from her brow. "Got it! Anything else, ma'am?"

"No, that'll be all, dear. Now where are Willow, Vulcan and Candy?"

CHAPTER 19

*T*here is something to be said for being a detective on some tropical island, like the detective who habitually solves cases on *Death in Paradise*. He can go about his business, uninterrupted by anyone but a few local coppers, and has, to a large extent, the last word on law and order. Darian, on the other hand, had a boatload of superiors to consider, and never did he appreciate this fact more than he did now, after arresting Nicolle Livermore.

He'd known he'd land himself in the center of a genuine crisis the moment word got out about this arrest, and he hadn't been mistaken. As long as he dabbled in mere killers and burglars and the occasional white collar criminal, things ticked over nicely, but as soon as he laid a hand on the wife of the future Prime Minister, all hell broke loose. Not only had he already been summoned upstairs by the commissioner, but the press had gone absolutely bonkers over the news.

Articles were popping up at a surprising speed about Nicolle Livermore being arrested and charged with kidnapping and attempted murder of the Wraith Wranglers, a fact which sparked a frenzied hullaballoo. Obviously the combination of the theft of the Pink Eulalie, the Smelt will and the connection with the Wraith Wranglers captured the imagination of the population and had Fleet Street's jaded newshounds foaming at the mouth.

The commissioner had told him he'd made a grave mistake. However, when he'd supplied the facts of the case had quickly backed down. It was irrefutable that Nicolle Livermore had threatened the Wraith Wranglers, had locked them up in the broom cupboard, and had made threats against their lives. Why she'd done it was anyone's guess, but that she had done it was certain. He had three witnesses, and once he got a hold of Pia Livermore, perhaps even four. Nicolle, of course, denied all charges, but they'd found the gun on her person, her fingerprints on the gun and a nice round hole in the ceiling, where the bullet had torn through on its way to the attic, where ballistics experts had dug it out of a nice Edwardian armoire.

Still, the commissioner had made it clear he wanted Nicolle released, the evidence be damned. It was obvious to anyone that the woman had simply lost it when suddenly harassed by these so-called ghost hunters. Anyone who'd ever been visited by a door-to-door salesman or even a couple of Jehovah's Witnesses could certainly sympathize with the poor woman. They'd probably imposed themselves on her to such an extent that she'd had no other recourse but to threaten them with violence if they didn't clear off.

And Darian had just returned to his office, feeling as if he'd just been sandbagged, when he was notified the Queen's secretary wanted a word. Mabel Swainston, when she was finally transferred, quickly made it clear her views pertaining to the case were in line with Scotland Yard brass. In short:

release Nicolle Livermore at once, arrest the Wraith Wranglers, and focus all his attention on finding the Pink Eulalie and the Smelt will.

"Furthermore, Her Royal Highness would like the contents of the Smelt will to be leaked to the media at the earliest possible convenience, Inspector."

"Um, could you repeat that last part?" he asked, sure he'd misheard.

"The Smelt will has been giving rise to all manner of outrageous rumor and speculation, and Her Majesty would like to put an end to all of that."

"You mean..."

"Her Majesty feels it is quite impossible for the will of her dear cousin to stipulate that Nathan Livermore is supposed to be the next Prime Minister, Inspector. She feels very strongly that Victoria Smelt would never have given those instructions. What we need to do is squash this hoax once and for all."

"A hoax perpetrated by..."

"By Livermore himself, most likely," said Mabel. "To further his career."

"But if we make the contents of the will public, and there is, as you suggest, no mention of any, shall we say, career advice for Miss Smelt's grandnephew, it will absolutely ruin the man's chances of becoming PM."

"Then so be it. Her Royal Majesty isn't in the business of creating political careers, Inspector, let that be absolutely clear. The United Kingdom is a democracy, and Her Majesty wants it to be known she doesn't choose the Prime Minister any more than she chooses who will represent us in the Eurovision Song Contest or the Olympic Games. So please find the will, leak it, and put an end to this idle speculation, in the process restoring Victoria Smelt's reputation who, I'm sure, never wanted any part of this nonsense."

The message was perfectly clear, and Darian said as much.

"Very well, then. I wish you good day, Inspector Watley. And remember, we never had this conversation, is that understood?"

"You have my word," he said. He wouldn't dream of discussing this with anyone. After Mabel had hung up, he sat motionless for the space of perhaps five minutes, mulling things over. He now found himself in a difficult position. He didn't want to release Nicolle, and he didn't want to arrest the Wraith Wranglers, obviously, but he didn't see how he had a choice.

He was pondering another matter, one he hadn't even discussed with the commissioner. Harry had told him Noble Dingles was murdered by a police officer, and after showing him a few pictures, he'd identified his killer as Worth Noon, a constable who'd only been in the service for about a year. Before, as it turned out, he'd been employed by a private security company, which often had dealings with the Ministry of Defense and... the Russian Embassy... So had the man worked for Nathan in the past? And why would Nathan have Dingles murdered? That simply made absolutely no sense.

And then there were the allegations that Nicolle Livermore was a Russian spy, simply because Dingles had once seen her leave the Russian embassy. Lots of people, he was sure, visited the Russian embassy. Perhaps she wanted to take a trip to Moscow and needed a visa? It certainly didn't automatically imply that she was a Russian spy, as Dingles seemed to believe.

Still, it added to the miasma of peculiarity that surrounded this case, and his gut told him there was a lot more to it than they'd uncovered so far.

As he released Nicolle Livermore from the holding cell,

he told her, "Please don't go firing any more guns at your visitors, Nicolle."

She gave him a sweet smile. "I'm so sorry, Darian," she said, placing her hand on his arm. "It's just that these Wraith Wranglers simply wouldn't leave well enough alone. They infuriated me so much I simply lost my head."

He nodded. She'd told him in her statement she'd asked the Wraith Wranglers to leave when they'd showed up on her doorstep unannounced, presenting her with an outrageous bill for their services of the previous night. She'd told them there was no way she was going to pay them ten thousand pounds simply for messing around and pretending to talk to ghosts, and that her husband had been right about them all along. They had then threatened to unleash even more poltergeists on her if she didn't pay, at which point an argument had ensued and she'd taken matters into her own hands by threatening them with a gun if they didn't leave the house, and had fired one warning shot into the ceiling, simply because they left her no choice.

Asked why she'd locked them up in the broom cupboard she said she planned to notify the police and have them arrested, after talking to her husband, but they'd somehow managed to escape and overpower her.

Her explanation sounded plausible enough, especially in light of the fact that the Wraith Wranglers weren't exactly your regular outfit, and had been courting controversy with their outlandish claims they could speak to ghosts.

Darian knew Nicolle was lying, but couldn't prove it. Nor could he put in his report that the Wraith Wranglers were for real. He'd be the laughing stock of the force, not to mention fired before the ink on his report was dry.

So he had no other choice than to watch Nicolle stride from the building, and call Harry to let her know that she had to watch her back. He balked at arresting her, even if the Queen herself had requested it, but knew she and Jarrett and Deshawn were fair game now, if only in the eyes of the tabloids.

CHAPTER 20

*H*arry, Jarrett and Deshawn were on their way back to Jarrett's when Darian's call came in. They'd been discussing what their next move should be, now that Nicolle was arrested, and now discovered things had suddenly taken a turn for the worse. When Harry disconnected, she wasn't smiling.

"What is it?" asked Jarrett.

"They want us arrested."

Jarrett frowned. "You're speaking in riddles. Who wants to arrest us?"

"The Queen."

"She does? I didn't know Her Highness had joined the Mounted Branch. She's quite the equestrian, you know. Loves her horses, she does."

"I'm not joking, Jarrett. The Queen wants the Wraith Wranglers gone. She thinks we're a disgrace to the country, and wants us put behind bars."

Jarrett laughed a careless laugh. "I'm sure Darian was pulling your leg as usual, Harry. I just happen to know the

Queen is one of my biggest fans. When I was running Air Zephyr, I was even in negotiations with the Palace to take the Prince Consort up into space. Said he'd always wanted to see the world from a different perspective. Of course the whole thing had to be called off when Jarrett I crash-landed and was destroyed, but relations have remained cordial, should I ever venture into the space travel business again."

"Well, she just asked Darian to arrest us," said Harry with a shrug. "So now might be a good time to get in touch with your old pal the Prince and ask him to have a quiet word with his wife. Darian isn't going to arrest us," she added when Jarrett stared at her with astonishment. "But that doesn't mean someone else won't, if the Queen starts throwing her weight about."

Jarrett darted a quick look through the window, as if expecting heavily trained and armed SAS commandos to come rappelling down from helicopters, prepared to take them down with the use of maximum force. So far, however, there were no heavy thumps on the car roof, indicating the SAS had landed, and no commandos in sight, so he said, "She can't do that."

"Well, apparently she can exert her influence and convey her wishes. That doesn't mean the police will act accordingly, but we still have to watch our backs, Darian said, and probably lay low for a while. Disband the Wraith Wranglers, and definitely keep a low profile until this whole thing blows over."

"But we can't do that!" he cried. "We can't simply disband the Wraith Wranglers just because Her Royal Highness is upset with us. Why is that, actually?" he added, interested. "Doesn't she like our work?"

"The Livermores. Nicolle Livermore has managed to convince everybody that she's the victim of abuse from the

Wraith Wranglers, and that she merely lost her cool when we refused to leave the house when she told us to."

Jarrett sat back, looking shell-shocked. "But that's an outrage!"

"She claims we tried to make her pay ten thousand quid for our services, and when she refused to pay, we threatened to unleash more poltergeists on her." She held up her arms. "Because hey, that's just the way we roll."

"We didn't charge a penny! I bankroll the entire operation!"

"Yes, you do, but apparently that's not how she told the story."

"And they believed her?"

"Who do you think they're going to believe, Jarrett? The wife of the future Prime Minister, or a bunch of weird Wraith Wrangling psychos?"

"Well, when you put it that way," he said, musingly.

"I think we better do what Darian says and keep a low profile. At least until this whole Livermore drama blows over."

"It won't blow over unless we blow this entire case wide open," he countered. "Nicolle Livermore is a Russian spy, and I'm not sure Nathan doesn't work for the Russians as well, trying to get him appointed to the highest post this country has to offer. This thing is bigger than the Cambridge Five, Harry, the biggest spy scandal ever to rock the nation. And I can't believe a boyhood chum of mine has gone over to the dark side!"

"I thought Nathan wasn't a chum of yours?"

"In a manner of speaking."

"But why murder Noble? Darian told me Noble's murderer used to work for a private security firm hired by the MOD *and* the Russian Embassy, so there's definitely a connection. But why? Could it be the Livermores discovered Noble suspected them of treason and had him silenced?"

"But why would Nicolle hire ghost hunters to get rid of Noble? She must have known that we were going to find out more than she wanted us to."

"She never expected us to actually get in contact with Noble," Harry ventured. "She probably thought we would simply cleanse the place. Burn some incense and chant some New Age songs and make the negative energy go away. Nobody really believes in actual ghosts, Jarrett. She just wanted to stop the weird noises and the moving furniture and the knocking doors. She probably didn't even know it was Noble doing all of that stuff."

"You know what I find strange?"

"Pretty much everything about this case?"

"Yes, but apart from that, why would the Livermores move into Noble's house? The man they had killed? It's a weird coincidence, don't you think?"

"They must have had their reasons," said Harry after a moment's thought. But Jarrett was right. It was weird, and she wondered why they'd done it.

"Pity Nate won't take my calls," said Jarrett. "I could have asked him."

"I think it's safe to say they won't invite you to their dinner parties anymore."

"Well, that's fine. I never liked them anyway. Very tedious conversations. All politics, politics, politics. As if I care a hoot about the future of our nation."

Harry grinned. Jarrett was probably the least politically-minded person she knew, which was refreshing, at a time when everything seemed to be about politics all the time. "So where are we going now?" she finally asked.

"Might I make a suggestion?" Deshawn piped up from the front seat.

"Yes, Deshawn," said Jarrett. "Suggest away, for we're fresh out of ideas right now. Aren't we, Harry?"

"We certainly are," she said, chewing her bottom lip. If the Queen wanted them locked up behind bars, and Nathan Livermore, the next Prime Minister of England, had it in for them, that was the end of the Wraith Wranglers.

"Why don't we subject Fats Domino's garage to a thorough search?"

"The police went over that garage with a fine-tooth comb, Deshawn," said Jarrett. "If they didn't find anything, it's safe to say we won't either."

"Yes, even Buckley struck out," said Harry.

"It was merely a suggestion," said Deshawn, expertly steering the Rolls through London traffic with the ease of one who's chauffeured half a million pound cars all his life. "If we should find ourselves in possession of the Pink Eulalie and the Smelt documents, we would have a bargaining chip that might induce the Queen and Scotland Yard to drop all charges against us. And we will finally know whether Victoria Smelt intended Nathan Livermore to be the next person in charge of our government and can act accordingly."

Darian had told Harry the Queen wanted the Smelt will made public. She didn't believe for a moment that her cousin had earmarked her grandnephew for the highest post and seemed rather convinced that the man had constructed the story himself. Harry had to admit it was a clever ruse. It would also explain why he was so desperate to get his hands on that document. If exposed as a fraud, his political career was effectively over.

"Deshawn is right," she said now. "We should focus on getting our hands on that will. Then we can force Nathan to come clean. It's the only way. We need the leverage, Jarrett. The leverage of the diamond *and* the documents."

"I can see that. But how do you propose we find what no one else has?"

She thought about this for a moment, then said, "I think I have an idea."

$\mathcal{N}$ athan cursed inwardly. He didn't like it when things didn't go his way. It was one of his less attractive qualities and he was well aware of it. He was an impatient man, and when things went wrong, even stooped to belligerence. At least he had good reason to feel slighted, as all his hopes and dreams had suddenly gone phut, merely because Fate had singled out his home to be the subject of a burglary. It was hard to keep his emotions in check at the best of times, much harder when he felt he was the subject of a witch hunt.

He took a seat on the last bench of the upper deck of the double-decker and tried to relax. All around him, tourists were having a ball, snapping pictures and shooting videos of Westminster Abbey, the women no doubt imagining they were Kate, the men wishing they were William, here on their wedding day. His frown deepened, all this excited tittering setting his teeth even more on edge than they already were. The bus had stopped in front of Big Ben and the bright red vehicle picked up another passenger, who now made his way

GHOST SAVE THE QUEEN

upstairs and then, without deigning him a look, took the next seat.

He was a squat man with a boxer's nose, beetling brows and a pockmarked face. In spite of the heat of the day, he was clad in a trench coat.

"We can't keep meeting like this, Boris," Nathan now grumbled.

"Where do you want us to meet? At your office? Public places are the best, Nathan. So let's simply stick to the plan and not get all jittery."

"I'm not jittery," he shot back, but it was obvious that he was.

First Nicolle had called him to let him know the Wraith Wranglers were onto them. Apparently they'd been chatting with Noble Dingles's ghost, who'd apprised them of the fact that he'd been killed by a cop! To make matters worse, she'd held the Wraith Wranglers at gunpoint and had locked them up in the broom cupboard until they decided what to do with them.

And even as he was getting into his car, Pia had called, all atwitter, telling him Mum had been captured by these crazy Wraith Wranglers, and that she was firing shots into the ceiling! And as he was speeding home, Darian had delivered the final blow to his equanimity, letting him know Nicolle had been arrested, accused of attacking Harry McCabre and her cohorts and locking them up. It was obvious she was going through some kind of collapse or nervous breakdown, Darian had said, but unfortunately he had no other choice than to take her into custody. Threatening people with a gun simply wasn't done, nor was tying them up, gagging them, and locking them up.

"I need these Wraith Wranglers taken care of," he now told Boris. "They've become a nuisance, sticking their noses where they don't belong."

"Do you believe in ghosts, Nathan?" asked Boris, pursing his lips.

"I do, but I never thought our poltergeist would turn out to be Noble Dingles, the man we iced! He's been feeding them information and apparently was the one who told these burglars how to open my safe!"

"I saw my first ghost at seventeen," Boris continued, as if Nathan hadn't spoken. "And I've seen plenty since. In fact many of my former colleagues have contacted me—after they died—asking me all kinds of favors. To let their wives know where they kept their savings, or to tell them they shouldn't get involved with this guy or that guy. I just tell them to buzz off and leave me in peace. Ghosts should know their place, and not bother the living."

"My thoughts exactly. Noble Dingles is becoming a genuine threat."

"It's a pity that even when dead, he can't keep his big mouth shut."

"We need to get rid of these Wraith Wranglers, Boris. If not checked, they'll ruin the entire operation. They know too much already as it is."

It was surprising how much they'd discovered in such a short time. This guy Dingles was as much of a blabbermouth in death as he'd been in life. Nicolle should never have invited these ghost hunters into their home, but how was she to know they were for real?! And now it was too late to stop them. They knew. They probably knew everything Dingles knew, which was too much for their own good. So they had to be stopped. Permanently.

"Why don't you let me handle the Wraith Wranglers?" asked Boris.

"You mean..."

Boris nodded. "Better to give them the silencing treatment, don't you think?" he asked, chuckling quietly at his own little joke.

Nathan was too tense to crack a smile. "I think their death will attract a lot of unwanted attention," he said. "Attention we can't afford, Boris."

"Just think of the attention we'll get if they make their findings public."

He nodded. Boris was right. They couldn't afford not to take care of these meddlesome fools. They needed to be silenced, and silencing people happened to be Boris's specialty. "So be it," he finally said. "Pity, though."

Boris looked up for the first time. "Pity? Why?"

"They seem like nice people, and Harry McCabre is Darian's girlfriend."

"That's what you get when you start interfering with things you don't understand," the Russian grumbled. "Ghosts aren't cuddly creatures like in the movies, Nathan. They're not all Casper the Friendly Ghost. Getting involved with the dead is a nasty business, and often leads to a sticky end, which is exactly what these ghost hunters of yours are now going to find out."

"They're not my ghost hunters," he protested. "They were Nicolle's idea."

"Not one of her best ideas. In fact a very serious error of judgment."

"I did warn her not to involve outsiders in our business," he grunted.

Boris gave him a pat on the shoulder. "This is all behind us now, Nathan. The Wraith Wranglers are a thing of the past. What about the burglars?"

"They need handling as well," he said, and here he had fewer qualms.

"Where are they now?"

"Still in jail. As soon as they get out…"

"I'll handle them. Don't worry. I'll handle all of your little problems."

"Before you do, make sure you get the ring and the documents."

Boris smiled, displaying a row of uneven, yellowed teeth. "I have ways of making them talk, Nathan. You know that. They'll sing like cuckoos before I'm through with them."

"Canaries," he corrected. "They'll sing like canaries."

"I don't care what bird they will imitate, but they will definitely sing."

"Good. That concludes our business, I presume?"

He made to get up, but Boris placed a hand on his arm. "One moment. I want you to know that once I find the documents, I will destroy them."

"Wait, what? No, you can't do that," he said, greatly dismayed.

Boris wagged an impressive finger in his face. "You should have gotten rid of that will a long time ago, Nathan. It puts you in a very awkward position. If the contents of that will become public knowledge…"

"Look, she was my great-aunt, all right? I can't just destroy her will."

"Sentimentality has no place in our business," said Boris sternly, like a teacher lecturing a wayward child. "I will burn that will once and for all."

He nodded morosely. Boris was right, of course. Still, it wasn't a pleasant thought that his beloved great-aunt Victoria's final will and testament would soon be destroyed. But so be it. Their cause was greater than one person.

"So you will take care of these Wraith Wranglers?"

"Don't give them another thought, Nathan."

And with these words, the Russian quickly rose to his feet and made his way to the front of the bus with surprising agility for such a short, squat man. He descended the small staircase, and then was gone. And as Nathan looked back through the window, he saw that Boris was already getting into a black taxicab. A very efficient man, he thought, and not a little bit scary, too.

CHAPTER 22

"*Y*ou're going to do what?!" cried Darian.

"We're going into business with your burglars," repeated Harry. "They know where the stuff is so we'll make a deal and take it from there."

"Look, I can't let them walk, Harry. We caught them with the stolen goods and I've got a clear path to a conviction. This wasn't a first offense."

"Have they told you where the ring or the will are?"

"No, but…"

"See? They'll never tell you what you want to know, but they'll tell me."

"And why is that?"

"Because I'm going to put Buckley and Noble on the trail. And then I'm going to make them an offer they can't possibly refuse. You'll love it, Darian."

"Oh, God," he groaned, mussing up his hair again. He used to have perfectly coiffed hair, going for the clean-cut FBI look, but nowadays he looked more like a drowned rat. All thanks to a certain Harry McCabre.

"First you let them walk, and then we have them followed

by our resident ghosts. They'll lead us straight to the rock and the documents, and bam! We've got what we wanted! Isn't that great?"

"Sure. And how will you get your hands on the stuff?"

"Here it comes, Darian. Are you sitting?"

He placed his free hand on his chair and gripped it tightly. "Shoot."

"They're going to help us break into Buckingham Palace."

There was a momentary silence. Then he said, "Are you nuts?"

"I don't think so. Though I've never talked to a shrink." She laughed, and in spite of himself, he had to smile. She had one of those tinkling, infectious laughs that did much to give him an uncommon sense of happiness, even if what she said was absolutely crazy. "Just hear me out, Darian, honey."

"Why Buckingham Palace? Why drag the Queen into this mess?"

"You said so yourself that the Queen wants that will made public. And I'm sure she would appreciate getting her hands on the Pink Eulalie as well."

"You'll simply convince her that the Wraith Wranglers are a menace and should be kept under lock and key. Not that she needs much convincing, mind you. She already seems to feel you're a highly undesirable outfit."

"Well, then we'll simply have to convince her otherwise. And since I very much doubt whether she'd ever consent to giving us an audience, or invite us to her annual garden party, we'll just have to barge in unannounced."

"You'll never get in. That place is a genuine fortress."

"We'll have Fats, Chuck and Elvis, won't we? Professional burglars! Don't you see, Darian? It's the perfect plan! Absolutely foolproof!"

"It's the craziest plan I've ever heard. You'll never get

within a mile of the Queen. They'll stop you right at the gate."

"That's the beauty of it, Darian. We're not going through the gate."

"Look, this is crazy, honey. Don't do it, all right? In fact, why don't I simply talk to these crooks and see if they won't tell me what I need to know."

"They'll never give up the location of that rock. Have you forgotten that Domino has a sick girl at home? He needs the money. You said so yourself."

That was true enough. He'd talked to the girl's physician and he'd told him she was a lost case. Terminal. Fats was thinking about taking her to the States for some kind of experimental treatment that would cost him an arm and a leg as it wasn't covered by the NHS. Fats needed money, and lots of it.

He'd already talked to Fats, tried to convince him to give up the stone in exchange for some kind of reward but he wasn't buying.

"Who's going to pay for the operation? You? Out of your own pocket?"

After that he'd lapsed into silence again, and had refused to cooperate. And of course the other two idiots weren't talking either, even when offered a deal. They were loyal to Fats to a fault, which wasn't surprising, as Elvis was Domino's kid's godfather, and Chuck was her uncle, since he was married to the guy's sister. They were a merry band of crooks, and family, too.

No, if they were going to extract information from these guys they had to find some other way. Maybe Harry's idea wasn't so bad. Release them, have them followed, and see where they'd hidden the loot. He took a snap decision. "All right. I'll do it. I'll have them released. But you have to promise me that you'll stay away from Buckingham Palace. I don't want you anywhere near the place, not even to watch the changing of the guards. Because if you get yourself arrested, you're going away for a very long time. A very, very long time, you understand? And I won't be able to do a thing."

"I do, Darian, and I'll take your advice into consideration."

He groaned. "You're going to do it, aren't you?"

"Like I said, I'll think about it," she said, and then promptly disconnected.

He shook his head, then picked up the phone again, to arrange for Fats Domino's gang to be released. Pentonville Prison Governor Mac Bunyon took the news with his customary equanimity.

"Too bad, Inspector. I was hoping to have them at least for a couple of weeks. We're organizing a concert for the inmates and we were looking forward to Elvis giving us his best shot at *Jailhouse Rock*."

"He's not the real Elvis Presley, Bunyon," he grunted.

There was a pause, then the prison boss said, "Still, I'm sure it would have been a real treat."

CHAPTER 23

*F*ats was a happy man, his heart light and a spring in his step as he walked from jail. He didn't know why he'd been sprung, but sprung he'd been, and he wasn't the kind of person who looked a gift horse in the mouth. In fact he couldn't recall ever having looked a horse in the mouth, gift or otherwise. If it had behooved Scotland Yard to let him walk free, it wasn't up to him to question their sterling good sense. They'd bought his story hook, line and sinker, and he commended them for it.

He and his two colleagues had done the world a favor when they cleaned up the Livermore trash dump. Recycling was all the rage, nowadays, and they'd simply done their share. In fact he'd told his story with so much fervor and conviction, he was starting to believe it himself, like a character actor becoming the character. He now firmly believed he and his associates were leaving the world a better place for future generations. Saving the polar bears from perishing on those melting ice caps in the North or the South or wherever ice caps were located. He recycled. He brought his lightbulbs and his batteries and his old socks back to the store. He made sure he always brought his own baggie when shopping at Aldi or Waitrose, so as not to add to that massive Great Pacific Garbage Patch. And if he had the money to spare, he would definitely plant solar panels on the roof of his little garage.

And as he and his two associates shared a taxicab back to their base of operations, as he liked to call his garage, Chuck and Elvis were prattling away animatedly, looking forward to glugging down frothy pints of lager.

Fats, though the prospect of a bottle of lager greatly appealed to him after the strictly abstemious atmosphere of Pentonville Prison, was eager to see whether the Pink Eulalie was still where he put it, and the Smelt will.

When they finally arrived, he found to his elation that the stone was still there, but that his stash of nudie magazines had been tampered with. Some of them even had entire pages ripped out! Those blasted coppers. If you can't even trust the fuzz not to pinch your stuff, who can you trust?

"So what's next?" asked Chuck, putting his feet up and sipping a Stella.

"Yeah, what's next?" echoed Elvis, also enjoying a refreshing lager.

But Fats was too busy trying to retrieve the ring from one of the fluorescent lamps. It had been the only place he could think of when the coppers had raided his garage. He figured it was probably the last place they'd look, and he was right. Coppers, like most humans, like to look down when searching a room, not up, and since there was a nice little hole in the ceiling where the electrical wiring went, he'd simply popped the ring in there and hoped for the best. Now to get it out was another matter entirely...

Finally, after some expert poking, he managed, and held it against the light which had concealed it so well. "Marvelous," he muttered. "Simply marvelous. What's next?" he asked.

"Simple. We sell the stone and we offer the will to the tabloids. That'll make them think twice."

Who it was he'd make think twice, he didn't happen to mention.

"Sell the stone, boss?" asked Elvis. "I thought you said it couldn't be done? And we can't very well blackmail Livermore now, can we? Not after all the fuss with the fuzz."

He grinned. His time in jail had been well spent. He'd actually met a guy who knew a guy who was into buying and selling rare and expensive jewelry that was too hot to trade on the regular market, to rich folks who didn't care where it came from.

"Don't worry, lads," he said now, hooking his thumbs into his waistband. "I know someone who'll pay good money for this trinket. He's what you might call a celebrity supplier, in that he supplies to celebrities. Gives those golden gals and girls everything they fancy: drugs, booze... stolen luxury items. Word on the street—or rather in prison cell seventy-eight—is that the guy is willing to pay top pound for something like our Pink Eulalie."

"But these celebrities, won't they want to wear the Pink Eulalie? Show it off on their Instantgram?" asked Chuck now.

"Instagram," corrected Elvis.

"That's what I said. They'll wanna post pictures on their Instantgram and write about it on their Tweeter and their Fakebook. You know how crazy those stars are to blab about every little detail of their hapless lives, boss."

"Well, they won't be Instantgramming this, I can tell you," he said, holding up the Pink Eulalie. "Unless they want to Tweeter from the pokey."

"Why don't you hand over the ring, Sonny Boy?" a harsh voice suddenly grated.

Fats whirled around, but couldn't put a face to the voice,

as there was nothing but empty space where it had come from. "Where are you?!" he cried. "Show your face, you coward!"

And suddenly he was wondering if this wasn't some kind of police trick. He didn't think so. From his extensive acquaintance with London's finest he didn't credit them with so much intelligence to think up a scheme like this.

"Just hand me the stone and the documents and nobody will get hurt," the voice insisted, sounding just as nasty as before. Then, slowly but certainly, the figure of a man became visible. He was short and squat, with a prominent nose, but what stood out most about his appearance was a bloody gash just beneath his chin, as if at some point in time he'd had his throat slit. Blood was seeping from the wound, staining a nice white shirt.

Then, to his surprise, suddenly Chuck cried, "Noble! Is that you?"

"How are you, mate?" asked Elvis, equally pleased to see the man.

Noble, if that was who this was, turned to the two men. "Yes, it is me, as you can clearly see. And you two have been very busy, haven't you?"

"Yes, we have!" cried Elvis, moving over to clap the newcomer on the back. To Fats's extreme surprise, his hand went straight through him!

"This is Noble Dingles, Fats," explained Chuck. "He's the ghost we met when we did the Livermore place, remember? The guy who's always thirsty."

"Are you still thirsty, Noble?" asked Elvis solicitously. "If you are, have a drink on me." He held up his bottle of Stella.

"And me," said Chuck, also holding up his bottle.

"Hit me," said Noble, twin grins spreading across his features. But as both Chuck and Elvis helpfully poured beer down the man's gullet, it simply splattered down on the floor, without hitting his stomach. "Oh, shoot," he said as he looked down. "This just keeps happening!"

Fats was still staring, and he now hitched up his jaw, which had dropped to the floor. "What the hell are you?!"

"We told you, Fats. Noble here is a ghost," Chuck said cheerfully.

"And he's brought a friend," Elvis added as he pointed at a second figure.

This one had suddenly materialized next to Noble and looked equally ghostly. He was an old man with a shock of white hair and a face like a Hobbit. And he was smiling at him affectionately. "Fats. Long time no see."

"B-b-buckley?" he asked. "B-b-but I thought you were d-d-dead!"

"I am dead," said Buckley. "But that doesn't mean I'm gone."

"This can't be happening," Fats said as he rubbed his eyes. But when he looked again, Buckley was still there, and so was this Noble Dingles fellow.

"Well, it is happening," Buckley confirmed good-naturedly. "I work with the Wraith Wranglers these days, Fats, and so does my good friend Noble."

"Yes, and we've come to pick up that stuff you stole from the Livermores," said Dingles, still staring sadly at the puddle of beer at his feet.

"Hey, we stole that stuff fair and square, Noble!" cried Chuck.

"You even helped us—you encouraged us!" added Elvis.

"I know I did. But that was before."

"Before what?" asked Chuck.

"Before I met Harry and Jarrett. And Deshawn. And Buckley, of course. These guys want to help me. To solve my murder and help me move on."

Fats close his eyes and shook his head, hoping this would

all go away. But when he opened his eyes, Buckley was still smiling benignly at him, and Noble Dingles was still eyeing Chuck's beer bottle wistfully.

"I missed you, Buckley," he finally said, reluctantly accepting the unacceptable. "I had a nice antique to pawn the other day and I thought of you."

"Aw, that's so nice of you, Fats," said Buckley. "Now if you will simply hand me the stone and the documents I'd like to ask a favor of you."

"A favor!" he cried. "You want to steal my loot and you expect me to do you a favor?! Have you gone completely mental since you passed away?"

"Actually I know all about the reason you need this stone and these documents so much, Fats," said Buckley gently. "I know all about Sebastiane's illness and the operation you want to fund in the States."

He stared at the ghost. "You know about that?"

"Of course. And the first thing you need to know is that we're going to fund that operation. So you should feel no qualms about handing over the Pink Eulalie and the Smelt will—where is that will, by the way? I've searched this place top to bottom and so have the police and we haven't found a trace of it."

After a moment's deliberation, he walked over to the stack of nudie magazines on the kitchen table and picked up the one that featured Miss July 1984. He opened it to its centerfold, let it unfold, and out fell a sheaf of papers. "I guess the coppers didn't appreciate Miss July as much as I did."

"Nor do I think Dame Victoria Smelt would have appreciated the company," Buckley stated with a soft chortle. "Hand them over, will you?"

Fats stared at Buckley's outstretched hand. "What's the favor you want?"

Buckley retracted his hand. "Well, first of all, I want you to retire from this burglary business, Fats. And you, too, Chuck. Elvis." He was adopting a stricter tone now, indicating he wasn't fooling around, if he ever had.

"And why would I do that?" asked Fats defiantly as he fingered the ring.

Buckley smiled. "Because if you don't, Noble and I will haunt you every second of your life. And if that doesn't convince you, I have plenty of ghostly friends who will join us. As you can probably imagine, in its two-thousand-year history, London has become positively congested with ghosts."

"You wouldn't do a thing like that, Buckley," he said. "Not to a buddy."

"Oh, but I most certainly will," said Buckley grimly. "And as an extra incentive I might add that my good friend Harry McCabre, who runs the Wraith Wranglers, is Inspector Watley's girlfriend, and she was instrumental in your release from prison but can have you back inside in a jiffy."

"Where millions of ghosts will haunt you to within an inch of your life," Noble added with obvious glee.

"I don't get it," said Fats, a little fretfully. "Why are you doing this?"

"I was in the same situation you find yourself in now, Fats."

"Having to give up a lucrative career just because some nasty ghost says so?"

"I was a crook, plain and simple, handling stolen goods all my life. Only when I died I finally looked back and realized that that kind of life leads nowhere. It doesn't give you happiness, Fats. I have since found that true happiness lies in helping others. So now I want to help you and your team."

"No, thank you very much. I like my life just the way it is," Fats said.

"Yeah, I'm good," Chuck said.

"Me too," said Elvis. "I like my life just fine, Mr. Buckley."

"This is not a negotiation," said Buckley sternly. "This is an order."

"You don't get to boss me around," said Fats. "Besides, you don't have a sick kid who's gonna die if you don't collect half a million quid real soon."

"Like I said, you'll have the money," said Buckley. "On the condition you pull one last job. One last burglary."

"What job?" asked Fats, always on the lookout for a bigger score.

"We're going to break into Buckingham Palace. And deliver the Pink Eulalie and the Smelt papers to Her Majesty the Queen."

CHAPTER 24

$\mathcal{T}$he meeting took place at Em's place, as Jarrett thought it a little too conspicuous to host three convicted burglars at the Ritz-Carlton and Harry was always embarrassed to entertain people at her own modest little nook.

Besides, Em was a professional hostess, whose parties had been the talk of the town when she was still married to Darian's father. She loved to entertain, though usually her guests belonged to a slightly higher class than the Domino gang.

Harry hadn't been mistaken. The moment the three crooks had walked out of jail, they'd made a beeline for the loot, and had revealed the location of the Pink Eulalie to careful observers Buckley and Dingles. The two ghosts had struck up a firm friendship, sharing a similar past of being murdered in quite a brutal manner.

All the guests were now seated around Em's dinner table, and the three crooks, especially, looked a little out of their depth, which was understandable. Usually when they entered an apartment as nice and opulent as Em's, it was in the dead of night, their faces covered with stockings, and eager to steal as much as they could carry. And judging from the way Domino's eyes kept darting about the room, it was obvious he hadn't left his thieving ways behind him yet. Buckley had had the same inclination when he'd first set foot inside Em's apartment, sizing up her extensive art collection and making keen calculations in his mind how much they would go for.

"As Buckley has already explained to you, we need to break into Buckingham Palace, Mr. Domino," Harry said. "And we need your help."

The crook shook his head. "Can't be done. That place is a fortress."

"Well, it simply has to be done."

"Yes, you see, we are in a spot of bother," Jarrett explained. "The Queen wants us sent to prison, simply for being who we are."

"A bunch of losers?" asked Fats, a little nastily, Harry felt.

"No, Wraith Wranglers," Jarrett corrected him with a tolerant smile. "She seems to feel we take advantage of her subjects by pretending we can talk to ghosts, something she obviously doesn't believe in. And to prove we really can talk to ghosts, we would like to introduce her to our very own Buckley and, of course, the star of this particular show, Mr. Noble Dingles."

"And we would like to offer her a trade," Harry continued. "The Pink Eulalie and the Smelt will in exchange for her promise not to put us in jail."

"Furthermore, we would like to ask her to bestow upon our little business the Royal Warrant of Appointment," said Jarrett. "A nice boost it would be."

Harry stared at him. "Royal Warrant? Are you sure?"

"Of course," said Jarrett. "Just like *Abels Moving Services* or *J. Arbour and Sons,* I think ours is a business worth boosting, Harry. What," he added dramatically, "do Abel or J. Arbour have that we don't have? Nothing. In fact, I think it will be refreshing to grant the royal warrant to a ghost hunting operation. I don't think the Queen has one of those on her list yet. Chocolates and condiments? Yes. Champagne? Most certainly. But ghost hunters? Not a single one in sight. And I'm sure Buckingham Palace has plenty of ghosts that need hunting. Quite a few of them blue-blooded, I would imagine."

"What about my kid?" asked Fats, interrupting this harangue. "She doesn't need a royal pardon—or a royal warrant. She needs an operation."

"And we will make sure she gets one," said Harry.

"Who's going to pay for it? The Queen?"

"Yes. We'll suggest it as a reward for returning the Eulalie and the will."

Fats laughed a hacking laugh. "She'll be quick to do that, I'm sure."

"Well, she desperately wants the will, that much we know," said Harry. "And I'm sure she'll be happy to have her favorite cousin's ring back, so..."

"She'll have us all in prison before we so much as bob a curtsy," said Elvis.

"Exactly," grunted Fats, who seemed to share his associate's skepticism.

"No, she won't," said Jarrett. "If she does, we won't give her the ring or the will. Those two items are our bargaining chips, if you see what I mean."

"I see that you won't get within ten yards of her," said Fats.

"Well, that's where you come in," said Jarrett. "You're the professional."

"That I am," Fats agreed. "And I'm telling you Buckingham Palace is impenetrable."

"I think the word you're looking for is impregnable, Fats,"

said Chuck, who obviously knew his thesaurus. "Or perhaps even impassable."

"The word I want," said Fats heatedly, "is suicide!" It showed that even though he might be improvable, he definitely wasn't imperturbable.

"I think you're exaggerating," said Jarrett. "It's just a pile of bricks."

"A pile of bricks protected by a small army. Or do you think those funny-looking guards are put there just for show? They have assault rifles and they *will* shoot!"

"Well, I'm sure you'll find a way," Jarrett repeated, his confidence in Fats obviously a lot higher than the latter's confidence in himself.

"Because if we don't," said Harry, "your little girl will not be able to have her operation." She felt bad for using this tack, but they needed to get inside the palace, and they needed Fats to do it.

"Not to mention your favorite Wraith Wranglers will end up in prison," added Jarrett.

"I don't mind," muttered Elvis.

"Me neither," Chuck chimed in.

But Fats was thinking hard now. "If we do this, you'll pay for the operation?"

"If the Queen balks, which I can't imagine she would," said Jarrett, "then I'll pay for the operation myself. You have my personal guarantee."

Harry stared at him. They hadn't discussed this, and she thought it was absolutely wonderful for him to suggest this.

Fats didn't seem to feel the same way. "And who are you then, mate? Santa Claus?"

"I'm Jarrett Zephyr-Thornton, and my father is the richest man in England."

The three crooks stared at Jarrett with a newfound

appreciation, seeing him in an entirely different light. "Oh," said Fats. "Well, that's all right, then."

And in this spirit of mutual appreciation, the meeting was finally off to a good start. Harry would have added that if they pulled this off, she'd demand of the Queen that she withdrew her support of Nathan Livermore, and demanded an inquiry into the death of Noble Dingles. But that would lead them too far, and wouldn't hold the attention of her audience, which was already showing signs of restlessness. These men were men of action, she knew, not politicians used to spending hours discussing the details of some trade deal.

"I think that concludes this meeting," she said. "Now all we need to do is figure out which of the two hundred rooms in the palace is the Queen's."

And they were just about to figure this out, when Buckley suddenly shouted, "Get down! Get down now!" And as she felt herself being pressed to the floor by Buckley's ghostly hand, the window shattered, and she thought she heard a bullet whizzing through the air, and then it impacted on the statuette of a brace of angels, which exploded into a million little pieces.

"Oh, no, you don't!" she heard Buckley shout, and then she saw him and Noble streaking toward the open window, and she was left, shaken not stirred, like James Bond's favorite drink, wondering what just happened.

CHAPTER 25

*L*ying on the floor in Em's living room, Harry thought that surely this was the world's end those prepper people were always going on about. Now she wished she'd followed Mark Zuckerberg's example, who was building a bunker in New Zealand, for when the apocalypse was finally here.

Bullets pinged and smashed into the various little ornaments Em liked to use to liven the place up, made holes in the walls, and generally turned the nice apartment into a shooting gallery and them into sitting ducks.

Judging from Em's face, she didn't like it one bit, and neither did she.

Domino's gang were also cowering for cover, huddled together behind the sofa, even though she thought that in a profession as fraught with danger as theirs, they'd be used to being shot at by irate homeowners and the like.

"I'm not sure I like this," Jarrett intimated, crawling over to her.

"Me neither," she confessed. "Is this the end of the world, Jarrett?"

"Well, if it is, it's different from what I imagined."

"What did you imagine?"

"Well, some big spaceship wiping out the planet or something. Not these measly little bullets. At this rate, the world won't be destroyed for ages."

He was right, of course. If this was the end, it was a very inefficient way to go about it. In other words, Earth wasn't the target here. They were!

"Do you think it's Livermore again?" Jarrett asked, confirming this view.

"Livermore? But why would he want to kill us?!"

"The will, of course. He wants it, and he thinks we have it."

"The will! Of course!"

"That's what I said."

She'd totally forgotten about the document. It was imperative they find out if it was true that La Smelt wanted to make him the next PM or not. "We need to see what's in it," she said, searching around for the document. Then she saw it, lying on an antique rolltop desk in the corner, along with the ring.

"Um, not to want to rain on your parade, Harry, but don't you think it would be more prudent to wait until the bullets stop whizzing around our ears? I mean, I know this will is important to you, but so are our lives."

She agreed, and kept her head down. She hoped Buckley and Noble, whatever they did, would do it quickly, for she did not enjoy this experience. Even though she'd signed up to help ghosts, and had accepted that there might be danger involved, she didn't like to be shot at. Indiana Jones might like this kind of thing, and James Bond, of course, neither man batting an eye, but she was starting to feel profoundly ill at ease with the entire setup.

"We should call the police," she now said, the idea

suddenly occurring to her. It was what regular people did in this type of situation, she figured.

"I'm sure that one of the neighbors will have called them by now," Jarrett said. "When shots are fired, that's usually their first thought, I should imagine."

Then, suddenly, the barrage stopped as abruptly as it had started. For a moment, nobody moved, and then Harry raised her head slowly and carefully, taking a peek at the window through which the shots had come. She could see across the street, and thought she saw a figure hurrying away on the roof of the building. Was it the shooter? Had he been scared off?

Buckley and Noble came floating back in, and Buckley said, "It was the same guy who killed Noble."

"The policeman?" asked Harry.

"Yes, I recognized him immediately," Noble confirmed.

"Did he recognize you?" asked Jarrett, now also sticking his head out again, like a turtle after a rainstorm. "Because he stopped shooting," he explained when Noble frowned at him.

"I don't think he could see me, actually," said Noble. "What made him stop shooting was the poke in the snoot I gave him. Several pokes, actually."

"And that kick in the family jewels I supplied," Buckley added with grim satisfaction.

"Where was he?" asked Deshawn, always interested in the technical minutiae. And while Buckley led him to the window and pointed to the roof across the street, explaining his exact position and the direction in which he'd fled, Em surveyed the damage with a distraught expression on her face.

"My wonderful apartment!" she cried. "Who's going to pay for all this?!"

The window had been shot out, and the wall now looked like Swiss cheese. Remarkably, a good many shots had been grouped around an Andy Warhol style rendering of the face of Mr. Morris. It was obvious the shooter didn't like cats. It also surprised Harry to see that Em wasn't sniffling anymore, as if this bullet business had killed the bug that was ailing her.

"Is it over?" asked Fats Domino, sticking his head out from behind the sofa. Two more heads popped up beside him: Chuck and Elvis.

"Is he gone?" asked Chuck, looking terrified.

"I think so," said Elvis.

Harry thought she saw the reason they weren't used to being fired at. When they snuck into a home it was usually under the cover of darkness, after ascertaining the owners were away. They rarely courted actual danger.

"Yes, it's over," Harry assured them, and they heaved breaths of relief.

Mr. Morris himself now also came waddling over, mewling plaintively, and stroking against Em's leg. She picked him up. "Did that bad man shoot at you?" she asked. "Don't worry, darling, he's gone now. Everything is fine."

"Is this a regular thing with you Wraith Wranglers?" asked Fats, looking at Harry with awe and respect written all over his face.

"No, this is just—"

"Oh, yes," interrupted Jarrett. "We get shot at all the time. Par for the course, wouldn't you say, Harry?"

"Jeez," said Elvis. "If I'd known that it was going to be like this…"

"Don't worry," said Harry quickly, giving Jarrett a reproachful look. "The ghosts are always there to protect us. Like you just saw, Buckley looks out for us, and so does Noble."

The three crooks shared a look of interest. "We should

have a ghost on our team," Chuck now said, and the others nodded. "To be on the lookout."

"Two ghosts," Elvis specified. "One to guard the front and one the back."

They looked at Noble now, whom they'd obviously come to view as part of the team. "What say you, Noble Dingles?" asked Fats. "Join the team?"

Harry cleared her throat. "I thought Buckley made it clear we want you to stop burgling places? If you're going to work with us you have to reform."

They stared at her as if 'reform' was a dirty word.

"From now you'll be walking the straight and narrow, boys," said Jarrett.

"So you won't need any ghosts to be 'on the lookout,'" said Harry.

"Pity," said Elvis, who couldn't hide his disappointment.

"Yeah, what a shame," echoed Chuck. "Now that we've got a good thing going with Noble. Did I mention that he helped us burgle that safe? We couldn't have done it without you, Noble. No Pink Eulalie and no will."

"Thanks," said Noble, deeply touched. "But we'll still be friends, right? In fact, whenever you need a babysitter or something, I'm your ghost, guys."

"Thanks, Noble," muttered Elvis, though he'd obviously had greater and more ambitious plans for Noble than mere babysitting. Or even housesitting.

"We need to get out of here before the police show up," Jarrett said, striking the business note.

"Why?" asked Harry. "We were the ones being shot at, not the ones doing the shooting."

"We can't be seen with the three stooges here," said Jarrett, indicating Fats and his troupe. "Or with the Pink Eulalie and the Smelt documents."

"Oh. Right."

"Besides, I'm sure they'll think we're responsible for this, seeing as how they seem to think the Wraith Wranglers are some sort of criminal gang."

"I'm sure Darian will protect us," said Harry. "He knows the truth."

"Yes, he does. But will he be able to convince his superiors? I doubt it."

Jarrett was right, of course. "All right. Let's get going, then."

"Where to?" asked Em, gently putting down Mr. Morris.

"No, no. You're staying here, Em," said Harry. "It's bad enough they shot your place to smithereens, I don't want to involve you any further."

"But I like to be involved," she said. "It's... fun," she added, darting a pained look at the destroyed portrait of Mr. Morris, which hung in tethers.

"You better stay here, Mrs. Sheetenhelm," Deshawn said. "So you can explain to the police what happened."

"Oh, all right," she said, reluctantly. "But I want you to promise to be careful, and not get into any more trouble than I would, Harry. Promise?"

"I promise, Em," said Harry, giving her future mother-in-law a hug.

Police sirens were sounding, and Jarrett said, "We have to go. Now."

Moments later, they were exiting the building, hurrying toward the Rolls Royce, and were ushered into the car by Deshawn. The 'three stooges' darted admiring looks at the interior and then the car quickly pulled into traffic.

Just in time, as they passed half a dozen police cars speeding their way.

"Where to?" Deshawn asked.

"Let's go to my place," Harry suggested.

"Both the police and the bad guys know where you live,

Harry," Jarrett pointed out. "Unless you want Snuggles to be shot at, you better reconsider."

"Right," she said, thinking. "Your place, then?"

Jarrett shook his head adamantly. "The Ritz-Carlton frowns upon crazed gunmen being lured onto the premises by careless residents and causing damage. We have to find a place where Nathan's goons can't find us."

"I know a place," said Deshawn now.

And as the car rolled on with a reassuring purr, Harry took out the will. She was burning with curiosity to know what was in this highly important and extremely coveted document. And as she started reading, it soon became clear to her that there was absolutely no mention of any cabinet post for Nathan. A lot of different bequeaths to different family members, stipulating in minute detail who would get the jewels, the different houses, the clothes... In fact the entire document was an itemized list of possessions and their beneficiaries, but of a cabinet post there was, as she'd surmised, no mention.

No noblewoman would, upon her demise, steer the course of future cabinet formation, nor would the political class accept such meddling. She now wondered why this rumor had ever received any credence at all, as it was simply too ludicrous to believe. But that, of course, was the power of a rumor: once started, it took on a life of its own, and became more potent as time went on and its source was never invalidated.

Nathan must have believed that the simple spreading of the rumor would greatly improve his chances of becoming the PM, since people would start to believe that the Queen herself was in his corner, and push his candidacy.

"And? What did Dame Smelt leave good old Nate?" asked Jarrett.

"A tie clip," said Harry.

"A tie clip?" asked Jarrett with a laugh.

"Yes. It belonged to Victoria's late husband. A very nice clip, probably."

"Undoubtedly," said Jarrett.

"But still, just a clip."

"No mention of any political wheeling and dealing?"

"Not a word."

"So Nathan Livermore was never meant to become the next PM?" asked Noble, hovering near the car ceiling.

"Not according to this document," said Harry, tucking the will away.

"The Queen will be happy to hear it," said Jarrett. "I always got the impression she never liked that upstart Nathan Livermore much anyway."

It didn't take Deshawn long to steer the car to their final destination, and when they got there, and he announced they'd arrived, Harry was curious to see where he'd taken them. When she got out of the car, she saw they were parked in front of a stately mansion in a quiet street, lined with maple trees.

"Where are we?" she asked as the others climbed out of the Rolls.

"This is my ancestral home," said Deshawn proudly. "Generations of Littles were born and raised here. I'm sure we'll be perfectly safe."

The house was three stories high, a red-bricked structure that had stood the test of time. A little weather-beaten, but otherwise in fine fettle, it was boarded off with a spiked iron fence. They mounted the few stone steps, and Deshawn pressed his finger on the bell. A coarse voice demanded he state his business, but when he said, "It's me, Dad," the tone of the voice changed to a more welcoming, "Why didn't you say so?! Come in, come in!" The buzzer confirmed these words, and then they all filed in after Deshawn.

CHAPTER 26

*D*eshawn's father proved to be a bluff and hearty sort of guy, quite the opposite of Deshawn, though physically they had a lot in common, as they were both short and stocky. Deshawn's mother, on the other hand, was a soft-spoken, slight woman, and welcomed them into her home with open arms. She was visibly pleased to meet Jarrett, her son's employer, and gave him three kisses and a warm hug, which Jarrett returned with a courteous smile.

"I'm so glad you're all safe," she gushed as the entire group filed into the living room. Deshawn had just finished telling her about the attack on their lives, and she had run the gamut of emotions as he told his tale and told it well. When her son had announced he wished to venture into the world of butlering, she'd probably never envisioned one day he'd be shot at.

"We're all perfectly fine," said Deshawn reassuringly. "And I'm quite sure the police will do everything in their power to apprehend the foul miscreant."

"Well, I'm not so sure," said Jarrett now. "The police seem

to have a hard time distinguishing between the bad guys and the good ones in this case."

"As long as you're safe," said Mrs. Little, "I'm happy."

"You can stay here for as long as you like," said Mr. Little, darting a curious look at Domino's gang. "And your friends, too, of course," he added.

"Oh, right," said Deshawn. "Where are my manners? Fats, Chuck and Elvis, meet my parents. Mom, dad, meet Fats, Chuck and Elvis. They're a, um, recent addition to the Wraith Wranglers, and will help us solve the case."

Mr. Little frowned a little. "So you're fully invested in this ghost hunting business now?"

"I am," Deshawn confirmed, darting a quick look at his employer.

"Yes, Deshawn is by way of being the pillar upon which the Wraith Wranglers were built," Jarrett said. "Without him, we would be nowhere."

"And here I always thought you were merely Jarrett's valet, darling," said Mrs. Little, who seemed a little confused about this state of affairs.

"There comes a time in a man's life when he's faced with an important decision, Mrs. Little," said Jarrett, affecting a grave air. "This time has arrived for Deshawn. Can he stand on the sidelines while the battle for the future of our world has begun? Or will he join the fight and put his life on the line? I'm proud to say that Deshawn has decided to step up and join us."

"What Jarrett means," Harry was quick to explain, fearing the Littles hadn't understood a word, "is that Deshawn is so much more than a valet."

"Oh, but I know," said Mrs. Little. "He's also a chauffeur, a personal shopper, a butler, a chef, a servant and who knows what else. Are you quite sure they're paying you to do all this?" she asked with motherly solicitude.

"Yes, did you check with the union like I told you to?" asked Mr. Little.

"I did and everything is perfectly aboveboard," said Deshawn, cringing a little to be having this conversation in the presence of his employer.

"In fact," said Jarrett, "it will please you to hear that I've recently decided to terminate Deshawn's employment. This marks a bold new step in our ongoing relationship and you won't fail to appreciate its significance."

"You... what?!" cried Deshawn's parents in unison.

Deshawn, too, seemed taken aback by this news that he'd just been given the Donald Trump treatment. Jarrett hadn't actually uttered the words 'You're fired,' but it was obvious that that was the gist of what he'd just said.

"Yes," said Jarrett, seemingly unaware of the impact his words had made. "I'm putting an end to this awkwardness once and for all. Deshawn and I can't continue to go through life master and servant, boss and underling, lackey and scullion, lord and vassal. Not after the feelings we discovered we've been harboring for one another. From now on we'll be perfect equals."

"Oh, Jarrett," muttered Deshawn.

"Deshawn Little," Jarrett said determinedly, getting down on one knee and gazing up into a startled Deshawn's eyes, "will you make me the happiest man in England and, by extension, the universe, and be my husband? To have and to hold, to love and to cherish, in sickness and in health, for richer, for poorer, and to adopt a wonderful baby girl or boy from Malawi or any other country that accepts Visa, American Express or MasterCard?"

"Oh, Jarrett," Deshawn repeated, his lower lip trembling now.

"And to prove I'm not choosy, we can even adopt from

Belgium if you like," Jarrett continued. "Or from Scotland. But only if you insist."

Harry thought she'd never seen Deshawn so moved in all the time she'd known the stalwart servitor. But then it was a genuine Cinderella story, of course, or one of those billionaire romance stories you hear so much about. Hollywood, if they found out about this, would definitely turn it into a major motion picture starring Ryan Reynolds and Andrew Garfield or the like.

By contrast, Deshawn's mother and father looked like they were on the verge of a mental collapse as they stared at the scene, aghast, clutching at each other. It appeared that to them the scene wasn't reminiscent of a romantic movie at all, but rather something from *Hammer House of Horror*. It was obvious that Deshawn hadn't come out of the closet yet, or at least not out of his parents' closet, and the news that their son was about to link his lot to a person of the same gender appeared to come as something of a shock.

"Yes," Deshawn finally said. "Yes, I *will* marry you, Jarrett Zephyr-Thornton the Third. I will link my lot to yours and yes, I will join you in adopting from any country that carries the Elton John seal of approval."

Jarrett sprang to his feet, and there followed one of those scenes where young readers are advised to close their eyes, as Jarrett and Deshawn locked lips and shared a genuine *Hallmark Channel* moment. A click sounded, and Harry saw that Elvis was taking snapshots with his smartphone, awkwardly wiping away a tear and saving the moment for posterity. Whether he also posted the pictures on Instantgram, Fakebook or Tweeter, Harry had no way of knowing, but she secretly hoped he did, for this was a precious moment.

Then, proving they were broad-minded as well as kind to strangers, Mr. and Mrs. Little, having recovered sufficiently from the shock of the surprise engagement, broke out the port—they hadn't had the forethought to stock up on champagne—and they all drank to the newly engaged couple's health.

How Jarrett was going to manage without his trusty valet/chauffeur/butler/chef/personal shopper/assistant, Harry didn't know, but she was sure he'd figure it out before the wedding bells finally rang out.

Unfortunately, there wasn't a lot of time to celebrate, for at that precise moment, Harry's phone demanded her attention and she saw it was Darian.

"Where are you?!" he practically yelled. After she told him they were safe and sound at the Littles, he simmered down. "I arrived here as soon as I could. Did you get a good look at the shooter?"

Harry had to wrench her mind back to the terrible events. Being surrounded by young love had done much to push the terrible events of the day to the background. "Yes," she said, before conceding, "No. I mean, Noble recognized him. It was the man who killed him, Darian. The same guy."

"Worth Noon," he grunted. "I sent a team to arrest the bastard after you told me about him and he's disappeared. He must have been working for Livermore all this time."

"I think this is much bigger than the Livermores." She quickly told him about the contents of the will, and he was pleased to discover that Nathan had fooled the world into believing he was The Chosen One. Selected by the establishment to rule the nation. And since the Queen can't go on record to voice her doubts, the rumor had been allowed to spread uncontested.

"So you have the will and the stone?" he asked.

"We have both, and we're going to deliver them to Her Majesty tonight."

There was a pause, and she thought Darian would vehemently protest, just like he had last time. But instead, he surprised her by saying, "I think you're one of the bravest people I know, Harry, and you have my full support."

"Thanks," she said, taken aback. "Um, aren't you going to get in trouble now that you've released the Domino gang?"

"I don't think so," he said. "The commissioner might not like the way I do things, but he trusts me, just like I trust you."

"Thanks," she repeated, after a pause. "That's very sweet of you, Darian."

"But promise me you'll be careful," he said, his voice turning husky.

"I will," she promised him.

CHAPTER 27

*P*eyton Thomas was having a hard time keeping his eyes open. His gizzard had been giving him trouble for the past couple of weeks, and the doctor had prescribed him some pills that had the side effect of making him drowsy. It was a bit of an inconvenience, as he was tasked to watch the CCTV monitors at the Buckingham Palace guard post, keeping an eye on possible intruders. He hadn't told his commanding officer about his troubles, for fear he'd take him off the job. He liked the guard post. It gave him the opportunity to be alone with his thoughts, and take the weight off his feet.

Foot Guard Thomas had large feet, which seemed made for standing guard, but he also carried around a rather large bulk, which made standing around all night a tough proposition. He was a large man with an imposing mustache, and as he adjusted his position, his chair creaked in protest.

He stared blankly at the bank of screens, depicting still lives of the palace perimeter where absolutely nothing was happening at the moment, and groaned, then rubbed his eyes and yawned cavernously. Nothing ever happened here, and why would it? Who in their right mind would try to break into Buckingham Palace of all places? You had to be absolutely barmy.

So he wasn't worried, and hoped the night would pass quickly. He had a date with a soft bed and could already envision his head hitting the pillow.

Fellow guard Justin Shelter ambled in, and took the seat next to him.

"And? How was movie night? You and Jane have a good time?"

Justin, a ruddy-faced man in his middle fifties, shook his head. "Absolutely blooming disaster, mate. Terrible, terrible film we picked."

"I thought you said it got raving reviews? Oscar nominations and all?"

"Oh, it got Oscar nominations up the hilt, mate, but that didn't make it a delight to watch. Anything but. The little woman cried all the way home."

"Didn't fancy it much, eh?"

"Hated it. Hated it like she hates piles. A regular weepfest, innit?"

Peyton shook his head. "And here I thought it was a musical comedy."

"That's what we thought. But it was one of them Oscar comedies. Where you go in expecting a laugh and you end up weeping like a teething tot."

"What was it called again?"

"*La La Land*. Great beginning. Rotten ending."

"Not a happy ending, eh?"

"Nope. It's not Bridget bloomin' Jones, innit? Happy endings are for suckers, apparently." He sighed. "Now it'll take me forever to get my wife to go and see a movie again. She hates weepies, but how was I to know?"

"Remind me never to see it," he said as he let his eyes drift across the screens. Suddenly, from the corner of his eye, he thought he saw movement where there wasn't supposed to be any movement. His eyes snapped to the screen in question. It was directed at the North-Eastern wall, which, topped with barbed wire, kept intruders out arriving from The Mall. Then, as he focused on the screen, suddenly it went blank, as if the feed had been cut.

He tapped it, then fiddled with the knobs, but nothing happened, and at that moment, the alarm started to blare. He jumped up, and so did Justin. But before they could react, it petered out again, ending with a whimper. And just then, the screen came back, displaying a crisp image of the wall. He peered at it keenly, but there was not an intruder in sight. So he settled back.

He shook his head. "Looks like the equipment is on the fritz again."

"What do you expect?" asked Justin. "Cutbacks. Always cutbacks."

CHAPTER 28

The switching off of the alarm had been Buckley's idea, as had the gag with the interference. As a ghost, he'd simply slipped inside the security system, and after fiddling around in there for a bit, had managed to disable it long enough for the small crew of burglars to scale the ten-foot fence and land safely on the other side. Now they were traversing the parkland surrounding the palace, and enjoying a nightly stroll across the smooth lawn.

The night was a perfect one for burgling, Harry felt, though she wasn't an expert, of course. The air was crisp and fresh, and the park was lit by a full moon that made the use of their flashlights unnecessary. And as she walked along, Jarrett by her side, she thought this felt just like a pleasant midnight stroll, and not the dangerous endeavor it really was.

"Nice night," she remarked.

"Very nice indeed," Jarrett agreed.

"Do you think the Queen is in?"

"I hope she is, otherwise we're in for a disappointment."

"The Queen," said Deshawn, "is in residence."

"How do you know?" asked Harry.

"He checked her Fakebook page, didn't he?" asked Chuck.

"The Royal Standard is flying above the residence," said Deshawn, pointing at a flag that was gently whipping in the breeze. "If the Queen is not in residence, the Union Jack would be flying."

"Wow, you know your royals, don't you, cocky?" asked Elvis admiringly.

"I have invested a little time in studying Her Royal Majesty's habits preparatory to our excursion," Deshawn confirmed.

"You make it sound like a school trip," grumbled Fats, who appeared to be in a foul mood. In direct contradiction to the old creed always to bring your good mood when going on a trip, he'd brought his foulest mood instead. Like any commanding officer, he preferred to stay far away from the battlefield, usually opting to direct his operatives from a safe distance. Now, however, he'd been forced to engage in direct combat along with the others, and he didn't like it one bit, judging from his continuous grumblings.

Deshawn had made a study of Buckingham Palace, trying to determine in which of the two hundred rooms the Queen might be sleeping, and had made an educated guess. So they now proceeded to the massive structure, looming up large before them, and soon arrived at a drainpipe that would hopefully take them to the right balcony. After a moment's deliberation, it was decided that Harry would be the first to make her way up and onto the balcony.

With some effort, she shimmied up the gleaming drain-pipe, which was outfitted with bolts at decent intervals, which made it easier to conquer. It wasn't long before she slipped her leg over the balcony wall and found herself facing French windows, one of which was open to a crack.

Her heart was beating in her throat now, as she patiently waited for the others to join her.

Jarrett was the next to arrive, and then Deshawn and then... nothing.

"Where are the others?" she asked in a stage whisper.

"Upon deliberation they have decided not to join us for a visit to the sovereign," said Deshawn. "They mentioned the words 'plausible deniability,' in case things go awry and we're apprehended by the Queen's Guard."

"What are they going to tell them? That they were going for a stroll and took a wrong turn?!" hissed Jarrett. "This is ridiculous!"

"They were adamant," said Deshawn.

Harry shrugged. "We'll manage without them from here on out."

And then she set foot for the French windows, behind which she hoped they would find the Queen, ready to listen to their story...

CHAPTER 29

*H*arry carefully placed her hand on the handle, and as she carefully opened the window, she braced herself for the blaring alarm. But there wasn't any, which meant they'd picked the right room. She stepped inside, her eyes adjusting to the darkness, and saw that a four-poster bed stood in the center of the relatively small room and in it, a person rested, sitting up.

"Hullo there," said Jarrett, stepping in behind Harry. "Anybody home?"

Instantly, there was movement, and Harry saw that the person slipped a sleeping mask off and then flicked on a lamp on the nightstand. They hadn't been mistaken: they were in the presence of royalty.

"Who are you?" cried the Queen, "and what are you doing in my room?"

She was dressed in a lime Liberty print nightgown, her silver hair covered in a hairnet, and as she placed her glasses on her face, she looked nonplussed.

"Hello there, Your Highness," said Jarrett good-naturedly. "You may remember me. Jarrett Zephyr-Thornton. I was going to take your husband up into space with me. The Zephyr? Only it crashed before we managed."

There was a pause, then the Queen said, "I do remember you, young man, but that doesn't answer my question. What on earth are you doing here?"

"Well, it's kind of a long story," said Jarrett. He turned to Harry. "This is my dear friend Henrietta McCabre. I'm sure she'll be able to explain everything a lot more succinctly than I ever could. Harry, you have the floor."

The Queen's scrutinizing gaze rested on Harry, then turned to Deshawn, who hadn't spoken. "And who are you?"

"That's my fiancé, ma'am," said Jarrett quickly. "Deshawn Little."

"It's an honor, Your Highness," said Deshawn, curtsying nicely.

The Queen gave him a slight nod. "So you're the famous Wraith Wranglers. And now you're wrangling wraiths at Buckingham Palace?"

"We came to give you this, Your Highness," said Harry, approaching the bed and handing the Queen the Pink Eulalie, which the monarch took with raised eyebrows. Then she handed her the sheaf of documents that constituted the last will and testament of the Queen's cousin. "We thought you might like to take a look at this. It's your cousin Victoria's will."

"So this is the famous will," murmured the Queen, after briefly studying the ring and placing it on her nightstand. She gave the will a quick perusal.

"There's nothing in it about Nathan Livermore being destined for the top cabinet job, ma'am," said Harry. "If that's what you're looking for."

"I knew it," said the Queen, in spite of herself.

"Yes, it appears good old Nate has fooled us all," said

Jarrett with a slight smile. He was hopping from one foot to the other, obviously a little jittery.

"Stand still, young man. You're making me dizzy," the Queen snapped.

"Sorry about that," muttered Jarrett, standing on one leg now.

"So that's why you came here?" asked the Queen. "To hand me this document?"

"And the Pink Eulalie."

"Yes, don't forget about the Pink Eulalie," said Jarrett. "We risked life and limb to get our hands on that thing."

"We wanted you to have the document, and we also wanted to ask you to look into a most disturbing matter, ma'am," said Harry.

The Queen eyed her censoriously but didn't speak.

"The thing is, we have reason to believe that Nathan Livermore isn't who he says he is." When the Queen still didn't speak, she trudged on. "You see, we... met the ghost of a man who was murdered, the man in whose house the Livermores now live, and that man, Noble Dingles, told us that Nathan Livermore's wife presumably is a Russian spy. We believe that it was this knowledge that cost him his life, for soon after he discovered this he was murdered. By a man who now works for Scotland Yard, but at the time was working for Nathan Livermore himself. This same man has tried to kill us today, presumably because we know too much as well."

"And don't forget about Nicolle Livermore attacking us," Jarrett said.

"Yes, Mrs. Livermore overheard me talking to the police about Noble, and the man he recognized as his killer. She threatened us, but we managed to overpower her and call the police."

"With the assistance of our ghostly companion, Buckley—

who's also a ghost—and Noble Dingles himself," said Jarrett, still standing on one leg.

"It's these facts we wanted to apprise you of, so that perhaps you can do something about it. If Nathan Livermore is a Russian spy, working for the Russian government, it would explain why he so desperately wanted to become the Prime Minister, spreading rumors about the Smelt will. As PM he would have access to all kinds of highly classified information, information he would then be able to hand to a foreign nation."

"These are serious accusations," said the Queen as she peered at Harry with glittering eyes. "And you say you have this information from a ghost?"

"I know how it sounds, ma'am," said Harry. "But yes, we are in contact with the ghost of Noble Dingles, and other ghosts as well, of course."

"Nonsense," snapped the sovereign. "I think I've heard enough. I thank you for bringing me the Pink Eulalie—if it's real, of course—and the will, but you are guilty of trespassing, and I think this has gone quite far enough."

She reached over to the nightstand to press a bell when suddenly from the window the ghostly form of Buckley drifted in, followed by Noble Dingles.

"One moment, ma'am," said Buckley as he floated over to the bed.

The Queen, staring up at him, uttered a little cry of dismay.

"What—what is this?!" she vociferated. "Who are you?!"

"My name is Sir Geoffrey Buckley, ma'am. And this is Noble Dingles, the man who was murdered on behalf of Nathan Livermore, to keep him quiet."

"But you're… ghosts!" said the Queen, her eyes now wide and fearful.

"There is nothing to fear, ma'am," said Harry quickly. "They're friends."

"I've been a part of the Wraith Wranglers from the start," said Buckley proudly. "And Noble is the victim in this case. As long as we don't bring his murderer to justice, he won't have peace. Which is why we've come to you."

The Queen was still staring, and her face had taken on a distinctly pale hue. Then she quickly reached over to the nightstand and pressed the bell.

Oh, no, Harry thought. Soon the place would be swarming with guards, and they would be arrested. Darian had been right. They were going to jail for a long time. Resignedly, she stood. "I'm sorry we barged in here like this," she said quietly. "We just thought…"

"What's all this?!" asked a voice from the door. "Where's the crisis?"

And when Harry looked up, she she saw they'd been joined by the Duke of Shropshire, the Queen's husband. He was clad in a burgundy housecoat with royal crest embroidered in gold, and looked amused at the strange sight that greeted his eyes upon entering the room. He was a sprightly old man, rail-thin and with military bearing, his eyes now sparkling curiously.

CHAPTER 30

"*H*ullo hullo hullo," said the newcomer, his hands clasped behind his back. "And what have we here? A party? Why wasn't I invited, bunny?"

"Ah, there you are, Pip," said the Queen. "I want you to meet the Wraith Wranglers. You know," she added irritably when he gave her a distinctly blank look, "the people who go about the place talking to ghosts."

"Oh, right. The nutters," he said, animation returning to his form. He took a few more paces and regarded Harry curiously. "So you're a Wraith Wrangler, eh? Seen a lot of ghosts, have you, then?"

"Oh, yes, sir, Your Highness," she said, uncertain how to address the Prince Consort. "In fact we've got two of them right here." She gestured at Buckley and Noble, who gave the prince a jolly wave, visibly impressed with their present company, and a little tongue-tied.

The Prince started violently at the sight of the two ghosts. "Oh, my," he muttered. "Sausage, it appears we have two ghostly visitors. Does that mean we've finally died and gone to heaven?"

"It appears so," she said primly. "So you can see them, too, can you, Pip?"

"Of course I can see them. I may be old but I'm not blind, woman."

"I thought as much," she said. "Let's try a little experiment, shall we?"

She got up and donned a puce dressing gown.

"What experiment?" the Prince asked, still staring at the ghosts as if he'd never seen anything like this before in his life, which probably he hadn't.

"Try to walk through them, Pip."

"What?!" he cried, looking aghast. "Are you batty?"

"Just walk through them. If they really are ghosts you should be able to."

"I know I should be able to, but I'm not going to! Who knows what kinds of diseases you can catch from walking through a ghost. Besides, I'm sure it's bad luck."

"Oh, no, sir, it really isn't," said Buckley. "In fact I'm sure it's good luck."

The Prince gestured at the ghost. "You don't think that if I walk through you, I'll drop dead, do you? And promptly turn into a ghost myself?"

"Far from it. In fact I'm sure you'll add several years to your life."

The Prince stared at the ghost, and seemed to consider this. Then, finally, he said, "Very well. At my age you take what you can get." And then he pottered in the direction of the ghost, and simply walked straight through him. Surprised how well this went, he then walked straight back again.

"Bunny!" he cried. "I did it. Did you see? I walked straight through that fellow!"

"I saw," she said, then tightened her dressing gown around her, and proceeded to follow in her husband's footsteps, marching through both Buckley and Noble. Both the

Queen and the Prince seemed to enjoy this game thoroughly, for they did it several times before the Queen said, with a wistful little sigh, "Now that was fun." She turned to Harry. "You proved your point, my dear. You really are a wraith wrangler and you really know how to handle your ghosts." To her husband, she added, "They brought me the Pink Eulalie."

"Splendid! Simply marvelous! What's the Pink Eulalie?"

"The Pink Eulalie!" she snapped. "The ring dear Victoria left to her grandnephew Nathan Livermore, who promptly gave it to his prostitute wife as an engagement ring. They're both Russian spies, you know."

"You don't say. I always thought there was something fishy about the fellow. It's in the eyes," he explained to Harry. "Shifty, if you know what I mean. Never looks a fellow straight in the eyes. A born politician."

"Yes, and there was absolutely no mention of Nathan in the will Victoria left," the Queen continued, handing the documents to the Prince now, who didn't seem to know what to do with them.

"What's this?" he asked, holding them out in front of him.

"Read it," she said.

He read it, and when he had, looked up. "So?"

"Did you see any mention of Victoria wanting Nathan to be the PM?"

"No, as a matter of fact I didn't. Should I have?"

"Well, if Nathan is to be believed, yes."

"So the blackguard was lying all this time," he said with a chuckle.

"Imagine that. Of course, I always thought as much. No one in their right mind would stipulate such a ridiculous clause in their will, and most certainly not Victoria, who was always the most sensible one in our family." She eyed Harry sharply now. "And you say that Nathan is working for the Russians?"

This time it was Noble's turn to pipe up. "I saw his wife leave the Russian embassy, a briefcase under her arm, and rumors always swirled around the ministry that she was Russian, or at least working for them."

"I see," she said ponderously. "This changes everything, of course."

"It does?" asked the Prince vaguely.

"Well, of course it does. We can't have members of our family working for a foreign government, can we? That's treason!"

"You're right," he said, nodding. "Treason. Can't have that, can we?"

"They tried to kill Harry and the others," said Buckley now.

"I'm the others," murmured Jarrett, for once not playing first fiddle.

"Who tried to kill Harry?" asked the Queen sharply.

"The same person who killed me," said Noble. "He works for Livermore."

"That's not good," said the Prince. "Not sporting. Can't have members of the royal family trying to kill you, my dear," he said, addressing Harry with a kindly smile. "It's simply not done." He peered at her through narrowed eyes. "You're awfully young to be a Wraith Wrangler, aren't you? I thought all you ghost hunters were old cockers like me. If you're as close to the grave as I am, talking to ghosts comes easy, I suppose. But you're still very much alive."

"That doesn't make any sense at all, Pip," said the Queen now. "You don't have to be on the verge of death to talk to the dead."

"No, but it helps, I suppose," he mused.

But then, before they could get into the more philosophical side of wraith wrangling, there was a loud commotion at the door, and suddenly two men burst in. One of them was Nathan Livermore, and the other was... the killer.

CHAPTER 31

"*N*athan!" cried the Queen, tugging her robe a bit tighter around herself. She probably felt she was underdressed to be receiving so many guests this night.

The Prince stood eyeing the newcomer with a nasty gleam in his eyes. "Nathan, my boy. What's all this I'm hearing about you being a Russian spy?"

Nathan's eyes darted to Jarrett, and he growled, "I see you've been spreading some nasty gossip about me, Jarrett, old man?"

"Quite the contrary, old chap," said Jarrett. "I've been showering you with compliments all night." Then he pointed at the second man, who was now holding a gun. The sight elicited cries of shock from the Queen and Harry. "You took your precautions. Were you afraid we were going to harm the Queen? Because if you were, I can promise you that harming even a single hair on her head was the furthest thing from our minds."

"What is that man doing here holding a gun?!" demanded the Queen.

Nathan grimaced. "I'm sorry about that, ma'am, but you

leave me no choice. I'm sure by now you've seen the will my great-aunt left?"

"Yes, I have. And I have to say I'm extremely disappointed in you. Spreading rumors about yourself all these years. What were you thinking?"

"He was thinking how to best serve those damn Russians!" cried the Prince, his hands shoved in the deep pockets of his robe, his eyes blazing.

"You guessed it," said Nathan. He spread his arms. "I confess! I am working for a foreign nation, and have been doing it for quite a long time!"

"But why?!" cried the Queen. "Why betray your own country?"

He shrugged. "Why not? They pay a great deal better than you ever did, ma'am. Oh, I know I should feel privileged to have been born into royalty, but unfortunately that title doesn't come with any money attached, does it? I had to work for a living all my life, and one does get tired of slaving away without having anything substantial to show for it."

"Money," spat the Prince contemptuously. "You're doing this for money?"

"Of course," said Nathan. "You can't imagine what it's like to have no money. It's not much fun, let me tell you, 'Pip.' And then suddenly Nicolle came along, and gave me to understand that if I really wanted to, I could have all the money in the world, and the lifestyle that goes with it, and all I had to do was follow instructions carefully and allow myself to be taken to the very top of the political food chain. So I thought to myself, why not?"

"Why not?" boomed the Prince. "Because you don't betray your own country. That sort of thing is simply not done!"

"Well, I've done it," he said. "And now I'm afraid we've arrived at the more unpleasant part of this evening's program." He gestured at the man with the gun. "Worth here has been dispatched by my employers to take care of the, um, shall we say, the heavy lifting?"

"What are you going to do?" asked the Queen, looking quite appalled.

"Don't do anything foolish, boy!" snapped the Prince. "You can still walk away from this."

"We both know that I can't," said Nathan. "Not since those annoying Wraith Wranglers started sticking their noses in. We should never have involved them. They made everything go wrong the moment they arrived."

"Don't do this, Nathan," urged Harry. "Don't throw your life away."

"If I don't, my life is over anyway, isn't it? Now I still have a chance."

"How did you get in here, anyway?" asked the Prince.

Nathan smiled. "The people I work for have a knack for hacking phones and internet connections. The moment Harry McCabre and her nosy parker friends started stirring up trouble they put her phone and computer under surveillance. It wasn't hard to figure out what they were up to, though when my contact told me they were breaking into the palace, I have to admit to being more than a little surprised. Of course the guards were quick to let me pass when I told them I had urgent business to discuss with my monarch."

The Duke of Shropshire darted a quick look at his wife, and then at the button next to the bed. She sidled up to it, but Nathan tsk-tsked.

"Don't move, ma'am. I don't object to the cavalry barging in here, but only after the deed is done." He nodded at his associate, who raised the gun.

"What do you intend to do?" asked the Queen, tilting her chin. "Murder us all?"

"Oh, no," said Nathan. "Nothing of the kind." He gestured

at Harry and Jarrett. "The Wraith Wranglers are going to murder you, of course. At which point Worth and I will come to the rescue and shoot them. Unfortunately we will arrive too late to save you. Your last words to me, which I will faithfully transmit to the media, will be to save our country from ruin by becoming PM. Which, of course, I will endeavor to do to the best of my abilities."

"Why would we murder the Queen?" asked Jarrett. "That's crazy!"

"But then you *are* crazy, aren't you, Jarrett? Or haven't you read the papers? All the tabloids are leading with the news that the Wraith Wranglers are a menace to society and should be outlawed. Even the serious papers are jumping into the fray. And believe me, after the Buckingham Palace massacre, you will all be world news. Unfortunately not for the right reasons." He laughed. "Now let's get this over with." He curtsied in the direction of the Queen. "I want you to know this hurts me more than you."

"I very much doubt that," she said grimly.

Just then, the Prince made a sudden leap forward, and tried to slap the gun away from Worth's hand. Unfortunately the man had anticipated this move, for he quickly turned and would have fired at the Prince Consort if not both Buckley and Noble hadn't suddenly streaked down on the man, and kicked the gun from his hands. The next moment, they were engaged in a fierce struggle, the ghosts trying to overpower the muscular goon.

"Oh, for heaven's sake," cried Nathan, picking up the gun. "Do I really have to do everything myself?" And then, with a determined look in his eyes, he turned on the Queen. But before he could pull the trigger, Harry accosted him, smacking her head into his midriff. The shot fired but it went wide, and then Nathan was pummeled to the floor,

Harry on top of him, and soon, with the help of Deshawn and Jarrett, was restrained, just like his killer friend.

The Queen quickly tripped over to her bedside, and triggered the alarm, and then it was wailing so loudly that it was as if all hell broke loose.

It wasn't long before the guards came charging in, and both Nathan and his lethal associate were placed under arrest and taken away.

When the guards proceeded to arrest Harry, Jarrett and Deshawn, the Prince interfered. "Hey, what do you think you're doing?"

"Arresting the Wraith Wranglers," said the Grenadier Guard. "These are the Wraith Wranglers, aren't they?" he asked, appearing confused.

"They are," confirmed the Queen. "And they're the ones who saved our lives tonight," she added with a kindly smile at Harry and the others.

Harry smiled back, and the guard left, shaking his head in confusion.

Just then, three heads came peeping over the balcony parapet. They belonged to Chuck, Elvis and Fats. "Hey!" said Chuck. "What's taking you so long?!" But then he caught sight of the Queen and the Prince and his eyes went wide. "Sorry, ma'am, sir," he said. "Didn't see you there."

"Are these friends of yours?" the Queen asked Harry.

"Yes, ma'am," said Harry. "They helped us scale the wall."

"Come in," said the Queen, making an imperial gesture with her hand. "The more the merrier."

The burglars trepidatiously walked in, curtsying before their sovereign.

"I'm sorry, ma'am," said Fats, blushing. "We didn't mean to startle you."

"No need to apologize. I was up. What is your role in this drama, sir?"

Briefly, Harry explained how they had started the ball rolling when they stole the Pink Eulalie and the will from the Livermore safe, and how they'd been instrumental in helping her and the others to break into the palace.

"It appears as if I owe you a great debt of gratitude, Mr. Domino," the Queen said after listening carefully to Harry's story. "And so does our country."

"Breaking into Buckingham Palace," said the Prince, shaking his head. "You men are simply loony."

"Yes, sir, we certainly are," confirmed Fats.

The Prince laughed a booming laugh. "I like these men, Sausage!"

The Queen's eyes were sparkling. "Yes, I rather think that I like them as well. Though the next time you want to share a great secret with me you might consider making an appointment through the proper channels."

"Yes, ma'am," said Elvis.

"Sorry about that, ma'am," added Chuck, bowing his head.

"It won't happen again," Fats assured her.

"See that it doesn't," she said sternly, and Harry was amazed how she managed to bring these three crooks to heel. Just then, a gaggle of Corgis and Dorgis came rushing in, yapping excitedly and jumping about the Queen's legs. She picked one up and petted it affectionately.

"There is one small favor we would like to ask of you, Your Majesty," said Harry now, and explained how Fats Domino's little girl was in urgent need of an operation that would cost close to half a million pounds.

"I'll take care of it," she said with typical alacrity.

"You mean…" said Fats, eyes wide as saucers now.

"We'll make sure your daughter is taken care of," she said kindly. "Now, if there is nothing else, I'd like to go back to bed if you don't mind."

"Yes, we do need our beauty sleep," the Prince chimed in.

"You don't get to our age by partying all night and having a ball."

"Of course," said Harry.

"We'll let you sleep now, sir," said Jarrett.

"Perhaps one minor point," said Deshawn, clearing his throat.

"Yes?" asked the Queen, giving him a stern look. "Who are you again?"

"He's my future husband, Your Majesty," said Jarrett proudly.

"Right. Well, speak up, young man. I don't have all night."

"The reputation of the Wraith Wranglers has received quite a nasty blow because of this whole Livermore affair, ma'am. And we were wondering if perhaps you would see fit to granting us a royal warrant?"

"Right," murmured Harry. In the commotion she'd forgotten all about that.

The Queen eyed Deshawn for a moment, her eyes glittering. Then she nodded curtly. "I can't grant you a royal warrant… yet, but I can offer to engage you and your team to work for us. Your work is exemplary, and the ghosts you handle have saved both mine and my husband's lives."

The Prince chuckled. "The press will have a field day."

"Serves them right for writing such nonsense about these wonderful people," said the Queen. "Once you've worked for us for five years, and have given satisfaction, we can talk about the Royal Warrant of Appointment."

"Thank you, ma'am," said Harry brokenly. This would really launch the Wraith Wranglers. Working for the royal family would put them on the map, and would make sure that their reputation would never be questioned again.

And she was just making her way back to the balcony, when the Queen sharply asked, "And where do you think you're going, young lady?"

"Back to where we came from?" she asked, confused.

"Back down the good old drainpipe," Jarrett added cheerfully. "Don't worry. We're getting the hang of it, ma'am. We'll be out of here in a jiffy."

"You will do nothing of the kind," she snapped. "You will go out the front door, holding your head high, not sneak out the backdoor like a bunch of common criminals." She motioned to one of the guards, who'd stayed behind to keep an eye on things. "Please escort them out the front gate, Peyton. And make sure they get home safely."

"Yes, ma'am," said the guard, looking a little puzzled.

Before they left the room, the Prince tapped Harry's shoulder lightly, and when she looked up, he said, with a twinkle in his eye, "Please come back soon. This place is infested with ghosts, I'm sure. Festooned with them."

"Oh, we will, sir," she said, quickly handing him her card.

He took it with a chuckle. "Though I'm sure that the next ghosts you will be called upon to kick out will be mine and hers. Isn't that right, Cabbage?"

"Oh, don't be silly, Pip," said the Queen. "We're going to be around for a very long time to come."

"But when we do go," he said with a sly smile, "we're going to haunt the hell out of this place, and whoever is unfortunate enough to come after us!"

EPILOGUE

The next few days were a flutter of activity, as the Wraith Wranglers were suddenly the talk of the town—or even the world. They had interviews to give, articles were being written about them, people suddenly had ghosts to get rid of across the nation, and their appointment book had never been as full as this. And all because of the Queen's insistence that from now on the Wraith Wranglers should be taken seriously.

Nathan Livermore was sentenced to a long stretch in prison after he'd confessed to his crimes. Treason was not considered a light matter, and both he and Worth were going away for a very long time. Nathan's handler, unfortunately, had suddenly been called back to Moscow, which vehemently denied the charges of espionage. They pointed out that Nathan was a very sick man, who'd been looking for attention in a very twisted way, and denied ever to have had any dealings with him whatsoever.

"What I still don't understand is why the Livermores decided to move into Noble's house," said Harry as she sat savoring a cup of coffee in Em's kitchen one morning a week after the stirring events at Buckingham Palace.

"Yes, that is a mystery," Em agreed.

Jarrett and Deshawn were currently in Venice, enjoying a quiet weekend, and were now probably riding a gondola, something Jarrett had always promised his former valet they'd do. They were taking a weekend off from their busy schedule and would be back on Monday.

"I think I might have the answer to that," said Darian.

Harry turned to him. "You do?"

Darian nodded as he savored his own cup of coffee. "We interviewed Pia, and even though she said she had no idea what her parents had been up to, she did give us an important clue. Apparently her dad had a special interest in the basement of the house, working on some project. We asked Nathan about it, but as usual he refused to cooperate, and so did Nicolle. So we did some digging ourselves. Turns out there's an old tunnel that leads from the Noble Dingles place to..."

"The Royal Palace?" asked Harry, excited.

Darian shook his head. "To the Russian Embassy. Apparently the house used to belong to a couple of Russian spies who lived there in the sixties and seventies. They'd found a way to deliver information to the embassy by using the tunnel. A low-fi way that was absolutely foolproof. When they were arrested, the tunnel was bricked up and consequently forgotten about. Except by the Russians, of course, who told Nathan Livermore about it."

"So Noble Dingles wasn't murdered because he saw Nicolle leave the Russian Embassy that day, but—"

He nodded. "But because the Livermores needed the house. Once Nathan was Prime Minister he'd have access to tons of information, and he needed a way to transfer it quickly and without being detected. He'd opened up the tunnel again, and was preparing to put it to good use, just like in the sixties."

"Poor Noble," said Harry. "Killed because he lived in the wrong house."

"At least now he knows why he died," said Darian.

He was right, of course. Now that Noble knew why he'd died, and his killer had been punished, he could finally get some closure and move on.

"What's going to happen to the Pink Eulalie?" asked Em.

"It will go into the royal collection," said Harry. "The Crown Jewels."

"So next time we want to see it we'll have to buy a ticket?"

"I guess so," said Harry. "Though I'm sure I could get you a discount." She gave Em a wink. "I know the person who goes over these things."

"So Jarrett and Deshawn are getting married, huh?" asked Em now, darting a keen look at her son.

"Yes, what about that?" he asked, oblivious.

Harry grinned at Em, who gave her an eyeroll. Darian might be an ace detective, but in some aspects of life he was completely clueless. Not that Harry was in a hurry to get married. She didn't even want to move in with Darian. In fact she liked things just the way they were, and had no intention of taking their budding relationship to the next level, as Em seemed to want.

Just then, the doorbell rang, and when Darian returned with Em's visitor, Harry saw that it was Broderick Watley, Darian's father and Em's ex-husband. Though judging from the kiss he gave her, it was obvious they were on very good terms. When Em looked up, and saw both Harry and Darian staring at her, she said, "Oh, please. Haven't you ever seen a kissing couple?"

Broderick, a thickset man with white mustache and buzz-cut, grinned. "Guess what? Em and I are getting married," he announced happily.

"Oh, God," groaned Darian.

"What?" asked Em. "Since when is marriage reserved for the young?"

"Since never," said Darian quickly. "In fact I think it's a great idea."

"So do I," said Harry, smiling from ear to ear. "This is so great! You guys should have done this ages ago!"

"Yes, well, we were too busy getting divorced," said Em with a smile.

"What about..." Darian halted when Em gave him a dark look.

"I had a long talk with Caroline, and she confessed to making the whole story about her and Broderick up. She was simply jealous of our happiness."

"Just like I always said," muttered Broderick, patting her hand.

"Yes, well, those pictures on her Facebook looked awfully real."

"Photoshop, darling. It's the scourge of the age. Though I did look rather buff in those pictures, didn't I? A regular George Clooney." She gave him the same look she'd directed at her son, and he quickly muttered, "Just saying."

"So are the Wraith Wranglers invited?" asked Harry.

"Of course, darling. You'll all be guests of honor. If not for you, Broderick and I would never have found each other." She clasped her ex-husband's hand firmly, who winced slightly.

"And the ghosts?" asked Darian with a twinkle in his eye. "Are they also invited?"

"Sure," said Broderick. "The good thing about ghosts is

that they don't cost you a penny. What?" he asked when they all stared at him. "It's true! They're the life and soul of the party and you don't have to feed them or stand them a drink. Saves you quite a packet. This is my second wedding, you know," he said defensively when Darian produced a critical snort. "You'd be surprised how expensive they can get. Cost you an arm and a leg."

"It will also be our last wedding," Em promised him, patting his hand.

"I should hope so," he said, looking proud and relieved.

"Am I invited?" suddenly a voice rang out.

"Buckley!" cried Em happily. "Of course you're invited!"

"As long as you don't eat or drink," muttered Darian.

"Oh, I won't," Buckley promised. "I gave all that up when I died."

"One advantage of being dead," said Broderick. "It's dirt cheap."

"Yes, it is," said Buckley. "Though there are disadvantages, too, I don't mind telling you."

"Oh?" asked Broderick, and as he and Buckley took a seat on the couch, the old ghost started telling him all about it.

Harry stared at them, and then back at Darian. "You never thought you'd see the day you'd be chatting away with ghosts, did you, honey?" she asked.

"No, I did not," he confirmed. "Though now that I am, I'm glad."

"You are?"

"Of course. If not for Buckley, we'd never have met."

She smiled. He was right. If not for Buckley being murdered, they'd never have met, and if not for Buckley's ghost, the Wraith Wranglers wouldn't have existed. They owed it all to the frizzy-haired, kind-faced little man who now sat pouring his lament into Broderick's receptive ear.

She raised her coffee cup, and so did Em and Darian. "To Buckley," she said.

"To Buckley," echoed Darian and Em.

"May he be with us for a very long time."

"Amen to that," said Darian.

EXCERPT FROM A TALE OF TWO HARRYS (GHOSTS OF LONDON 4)

Prologue

"And... Action!"

Harry Potter sat at the casino bar and nursed his whiskey —shaken, not stirred—while trying to look casual and debonair. In his tux with the crisply ironed white shirt and black slacks he was doing a pretty good job. This Monte Carlo casino was way swanky, and the baccarat table a buzz of activity as players dressed to impress crowded around the croupier.

One of the players was Hermione, and he watched her intently as she gave him the secret signal. He narrowed his eyes as he caught sight of Le Miffre at the poker table, the most dangerous criminal ever to walk the face of the earth. The dark-haired master evildoer was casually letting his chips fall where they might, and gave no sign he knew he was being watched.

Jacques Le Miffre had recently gone into business with Frank Riddle, the evil twin of Tom Riddle, also known as Lord Voldemort, and this was Harry, Hermione and Ron's attempt to catch the evil genius, who was building himself an army of followers to rival that of his twin brother.

Just then, Ron walked over, dressed in a frilly pink tux that looked absolutely ridiculous. Harry casually brought his hand to his mouth and muttered into his wrist mic, "Did Liberace have a garage sale, Ron?"

"It was the only bloody thing the Ministry of Espionage had left. It was either this or a lime-green one that used to belong to Kermit the Frog."

Ron joined Harry at the bar, and they both watched Le Miffre carefully. The criminal mastermind was tapping his chin, which was his tell, Harry knew. He shared a look of understanding with Hermione. Le Miffre was going to go all in now. Time to up their game and get in on the action. He casually got up and crossed the casino floor to the poker table.

"Mind if I join you?" he asked Le Miffre.

The evil genius gave him an appraising glance, then nodded. Harry sat down. Time to show Le Miffre who he was dealing with. It was do or die.

"Oh, Harry, do be careful," Hermione's voice trumpeted in his ear.

He locked eyes with the fair-haired beauty and nodded. "Always."

Just then, the ghost of a fat man came bursting through the table, upending the entire game and sending chips and cards flying everywhere.

"What the…" Harry cried, and even Le Miffre seemed miffed.

The ghost howled a startled cry, apparently as surprised as they were, and howled, "He killed me! The Dark Lord killed me! Killed me dead!"

"Cut!" the director yelled. "Cut! Cut! Cut! Cut! Cut!"

Myron Catling heaved a weary sigh and got up from his

seat to stretch his limbs. The young actor, chosen to follow in the footsteps of Daniel Radcliffe and play the legendary Harry Potter, was frankly getting sick and tired of this nonsense. This was the third time already that this poltergeist had interrupted his key scene, and he was losing his patience.

Devin Design, the actor who played Ron, walked over. "What's all this nonsense?! Why can't they get rid of this bloody nuisance?"

"It's not a nuisance, Devin," he said. "It's a poltergeist."

Devin laughed his trademark whinnying laugh, very different from the character he was playing, and a lot more annoying. "That's impossible! Ghosts don't exist!"

"Ghosts do exist, Devin," Christy Gyp said prissily. Christy had been selected from thousands of actors to step into Emma Watson's shoes as Hermione Granger, and was doing a good job of imitating the part she was supposed to play. "Can't you see? This poor soul probably died in this studio and now he's trapped here." She looked properly concerned as they all watched the poltergeist dive back into the table and disappear from sight, leaving a large glob of green goo on the poker table and on everyone who was so unfortunate to stand too close.

"Well, bloody hell!" Sam Carr cried. He played Le Miffre and was now covered from head to toe in the green slimy substance. "He slimed me!"

"It's ectoplasm," Christy said knowingly. "It's supposed to be great for your complexion." She dipped a finger into the slime and rubbed it across the back of her hand. "Has both exfoliating and hydrating qualities."

The director stalked up to them. He was a rail-thin man in his mid-fifties and was famous for having directed more than a few James Bond movies. In fact most of the people working on the new Harry Potter movie—*Harry Potter and the Dark Lord's Return*—were veterans of the James Bond franchise. They'd even rehashed an old James Bond script.

"This is the third time today that horrible beast has done this!" the director fumed. He stared at the table, which was now a mess. "We're going to have to get the set decorators in here and redo the entire set. Again!"

There were groans of exasperation from the extras who played the other casino guests and players. They'd been on their feet for hours, trying to get this scene right. Myron wasn't too well pleased either. He was starting to lose his focus, and since this was a breakout part for him, he couldn't exactly afford to drop the ball. He was, after all, playing the lead.

"Can't we film this scene another time?" he asked. "Maybe move on to the next scene on the schedule for now?"

"No way," said the director, upsetting his tousled head of gray hair. "The next scene requires even more preparation. It's the scene where Le Miffre tortures you in the casino basement and Hermione and Ron save your life by knocking him out with the Hellfire curse."

Yep. The script wasn't exactly adapted from a JK Rowling book.

Just then, Myron's eyes were drawn to the ceiling, where a crimson spot had appeared. He pointed at it. "Has that always been there?"

The others' eyes also rose to check out the spot.

"I think it's more of that slime," Devin said.

"Ectoplasm," Christy corrected him.

"Whatever. I just think this whole thing is a joke. Something cooked up by the marketing department to drum up interest for the movie."

"Yeah, because a new Harry Potter movie needs all the interest it can get," Christy said with an eyeroll.

In the movie, Ron and Hermione might be an item now,

but their actors didn't exactly get along. Not that Myron blamed Devin. Christy could be a pain in the butt sometimes. She was a method actress, and liked to stay in character between scenes. And Hermione might be lovely in the movies—or the books—but in real life her know-it-all act could be grating.

The table moved again, and the ghost popped back out. "He killed me!" he was yelling. "The Dark Lord killed me! He killed me dead!"

"Yeah, yeah, yeah," Devin said. "You said that already. Your stupid little party trick is getting old, buddy."

The ghost hovered over the poker table for a moment, taking in Devin, Myron and Christy, then said, "Save me, Harry Potter. Save me!"

But instead of sticking around to be saved, he streaked into the ceiling, spraying them all with more goo. As if that wasn't bad enough, he slammed into the ceiling so hard it burst open and something big and heavy dropped out! It landed smack dab in the middle of the table and, finally giving up the fight, the table collapsed and smashed to the floor.

"What the hell…" Myron said as he stared down at whatever had dropped out of the ceiling. And then Christy started to scream, and he saw what it was: the body of a very large, very dead man. A man who was the spitting image of the ghost.

Chapter One

I picked up my phone and saw I had three missed messages from Darian. I was hurrying after Jarrett as we walked past the guard station and into the studio. Pinewood Studios is famous for the James Bond movies, just like Leavesden Studios is famous for the Harry Potter movies.

Why they were filming the ninth Potter movie here, I didn't know, nor did I care.

We'd been called here to do a job. Ever since Jarrett Zephyr-Thornton and I—Jarrett is my best friend and associate—launched the Wraith Wranglers, our brand of ghost hunting had been in high demand, but this was by far our highest-profile job ever. We'd never been called in to drive away a ghost on the set of a major motion picture before.

"Do you think Harry Potter will be there?" Jarrett asked excitedly as we were led through a maze of corridors and sets to the main soundstage.

"I'm sure they'll all be there," I said. I was more concerned with Darian and why he'd left those messages right now. I hadn't seen the Scotland Yard inspector in a couple of days, nor had I heard from him, and I was starting to wonder what was going on. Ever since we started dating, not a day had gone by when we hadn't spoken on the phone or met either at his place or mine. I was starting to think he'd met someone new.

"I can't wait to meet Hermione Granger," Jarrett said. "She's the bomb."

Oh, in case you were wondering, my name is Henrietta 'Harry' McCabre. I'm a twenty-three-year-old former antique store clerk who'd inadvertently landed a job as a ghost hunter when my former employer Sir Geoffrey Buckley was murdered. His ghost had come back to help me solve his murder, and from there Jarrett and I had gone on to solve more ghost mysteries than anyone could shake a stick at. With my fair complexion, blond bob and golden eyes, I don't exactly look like a ghost hunter. Then again, what does a ghost hunter look like? I'd never met one before I became one.

Still, Jarrett might be closer to what people expect from a

ghost hunter. Fair-haired, lean, tan and lanky, he's one of England's richest men, perhaps even the richest. Well, technically his father is the billionaire in the family, but since Jarrett stands to inherit the bulk of his father's fortune one day, that's probably a minor point of contention.

I'd gotten the call when I was feeding an aspirin to my snowy white Persian Snuggles. Snuggles has the flu, and an aspirin was what the doctor ordered. I'd almost dropped the pill—and Snuggles—when the phone rang and Jarrett announced the Wraith Wranglers were once again being called to the rescue.

We finally arrived at what was apparently the main soundstage, and I was properly impressed with how huge it was. Everywhere I looked I saw different sets. One that looked like a basement, another that could be the living room of the Dursley place on Privet Drive, and another that looked like Dumbledore's office. Yep, this was a Harry Potter movie all right.

"Oh, this is so cool!" Jarrett exclaimed, clapping his hands excitedly.

"So where is this ghost?" I asked the guard who'd led us here. He was a big and burly man with an impressive mustache that curled up at the edges.

"Right there, ma'am," he said, pointing at a small gathering of people on the set of a casino.

"Thanks," I said, taking Jarrett by the arm and dragging him along.

I saw one actor with round Harry Potter spectacles, and guessed that he was the lead, another one who faintly resembled Emma Watson, and a ginger-haired actor who could only be Rupert Grint's replacement. A very thin, very rattled-looking man stood pacing the scene, accompanied by a stern-looking woman, her hair tied back in a tight bun. The moment we arrived, they all turned to us.

"Are you the Wraith Wranglers?" the woman asked. She held out her hand. "Marsha Shalver. I'm the producer. Thank God you could make it."

"You even beat the cops," the thin man said.

"This is Nathan Gaberdine, the director." She quickly introduced the lead actors, and then led us to a mountain of a man who lay on top of a collapsed table.

"Oh, I recognize him!" Jarrett cried enthusiastically. "Hagrid, right?"

The producer eyed him reproachfully. "No, that's Uriel Pieres. Or at least it used to be, until he died and landed in the middle of our Monte Carlo set."

"He's dead?" Jarrett asked.

"Very astute of you," Marsha said wryly. "Yes, he's dead. It's his ghost that's been giving us so much trouble these past couple of days."

I bent down next to the body and immediately recoiled. He smelled terrible. "A couple of days, you said?"

The producer nodded. She had a clipboard pressed to her chest, and looked more like a script girl than a high-powered producer. She snatched up a pair of reading glasses dangling from a string around her neck and slipped them on, then read from her clipboard. "Uriel Pieres. Member of our cleaning crew. Didn't show up for duty last week. His supervisor figured he'd decided to quit on us."

"But instead someone stuffed him into the ceiling," Jarrett marveled, staring up at the large hole.

"It's not really a ceiling," the producer said. "It's part of the set. Whoever killed him must either have dragged his body up there to get rid of him, or maybe he was cleaning the crawl space and was killed up there. Whatever the case, his ghost has been holding up production. So if you could do... whatever it is that you do, we'd all be very grateful."

"But won't the police shut down production?" I asked.

She laughed a curt laugh. "Not a chance. This is a multi-million-dollar production with a tight schedule and a winter release date set in stone. Nothing can shut down this production, and most definitely not the death of some hapless cleaner. And if that sounds harsh, that's too bad."

And with these words, she abruptly turned on her heel and strode off, leaving us to 'do our thing.'

"That did sound a little harsh," I said.

"I didn't even get to say hi to Harry Potter," Jarrett lamented.

"Harry Potter doesn't exist, Jarrett. He's a figment of someone's imagination. And that guy over there is just an actor playing a part."

"Ouch. Someone is feeling testy."

"I'm testy because Darian keeps sending me messages and when I call him he doesn't pick up his phone." I had no idea what was going on with the guy but I knew I didn't like it one bit.

"I think I know why he's not picking up his phone right now," Jarrett said, giving me a nudge. I turned in the direction he was facing, and saw a tall, broad-shouldered, strikingly handsome man stride into the studio. Darian Watley. He was following the same mustachioed guard who'd led us here. They were accompanied by a short, squat guy with sandy hair and deep-set beady black eyes. Darian himself easily towered over the man.

Darian Watley was the Scotland Yard inspector who'd investigated Sir Geoffrey Buckley's murder. He'd been a non-believer for a long time, claiming ghosts didn't exist... until he was slimed by one. Our relationship had known its ups and downs, and apparently right now we were going through a rough patch. At least judging by the way he was looking at me.

"He doesn't seem very happy to see us," Jarrett said.

"Nope, he does not."

"And who's the midget? I didn't know Darian had a partner?"

"He doesn't. Unless there's something he didn't tell me."

The police officers joined Marsha Shalver and the others, and she gave them the same spiel she'd given us. Darian kept darting dark looks at Jarrett and me, and so did his pint-sized partner.

"I don't think the new guy is a big fan of the Wraith Wranglers," Jarrett said. "Oh, goodie, they're coming over."

Darian and his partner joined us. "Harry," Darian said by way of greeting. He sounded very officious, as if we were total strangers.

"Hey, Darian. I'm sorry I didn't pick up. We were on our way over here, and I must have missed your calls. What did you want to tell me?"

The squat man with the deep-set eyes turned them on Darian. "What did I tell you, Watley? No more canoodling with the freaky ghost hunter."

This took me aback somewhat. "Um… what did you just call me?"

"This is Inspector Reto Slack," Darian said by way of introduction. "He's my new partner. Slack, meet Henrietta McCabre and Jarrett Zephyr-Thornton, also known as the Wraith Wranglers."

"I know who they are," Slack growled, his black eyes narrowed into slits. "What I would like to know is what the hell they are doing here."

"If you must know, we were invited," Jarrett said.

"By whom?"

"By me." Marsha had walked up to us. "I hired the Wraith Wranglers to get rid of the spooky pest that's been hounding our production for days."

"That's ridiculous," Inspector Slack grunted. "There's no

such thing as ghosts. I want these two idiots escorted from the premises. This is now a crime scene, and I'm not tolerating any intruders."

"Harry and Jarrett are here on my invitation, Inspector," Marsha said, her voice taking on a steely note. This was clearly a woman you didn't want to mess with. "And they're staying right here. If you don't like it, you can take it up with Prime Minister June. I don't have to remind me she's a very big Harry Potter fan, and very happy that we're shooting a new movie."

Slack twisted his face into a nasty grimace. "You can't do that."

"I can and I will. And now if you'll excuse me, I have a production to run. And you, I believe, have a murder to solve."

At this, she turned on her heel and stalked off in the direction of her director and main talent. The show must go on.

Slack gave me a warning glare. "I don't want you interfering with my investigation, is that understood?" Then he turned on Darian. "And I don't want you communicating with these Wraith Wranglers in any way, shape or form. Your job depends on it, Watley. Is that clear?"

"Crystal," Darian said between gritted teeth.

I gave him a questioning look but he totally ignored me and followed his partner as they distanced themselves and stalked over to the dead body on display. More police officers had arrived and they were marking off the crime scene with yellow crime scene tape.

"That was fun," Jarrett said. "I don't think I like your boyfriend's new friend."

"I don't like him either," I said, casting a concerned look at Darian. I didn't get it. Why all of a sudden did he pretend we hardly knew each other? And why was his new partner acting like his boss? Whatever the case, something wasn't right, and I was determined to find out what.

Chapter Two

"He can't do this," I said. "He can't just ignore me like this."

"Well, actually he can," Jarrett said. "He just did."

I cast a nasty glance back at the police inspector, who stood gazing down at the body of the man that had dropped from the ceiling. The coroner had arrived and was carefully examining the body.

I willed Darian to turn and look at me, but he steadfastly pretended not to notice. It was driving me crazy. "I don't get it," I said, turning away.

"It's this new craze," Jarrett opined. "It's called ghosting. One day you're happily rattling headboards, like lovers do, and the next they pretend like they don't know you. No messages, no phone calls, no emails. They simply cut off all communication. Ghosting. It's the latest trend."

"Well, it's not like he's cut off all communication. He did try to call."

"Probably to tell you not to call him again. Ever."

"Darian would never do that. He's a good guy."

"Honey, even good guys have their breaking point. Maybe it's something you said?" He ignored my death-ray look. "Or did? There must have been warning signs. There always are."

"Trust me, there was nothing. The last time I saw him was…" I thought back. Had it really been a week ago? Time flies by so fast when you're hunting ghosts. "Well, everything was fine. We went out to dinner and he talked about his mum and dad getting back together and maybe even getting married again."

"That's it. That's what decided him," Jarrett said. "A lot of men get scared off when their girlfriends bring up the M word. Marriage," he added in case I hadn't caught on.

"I didn't bring up the M word. He did. And he wasn't talking about our M. he was talking about Em and Broderick's upcoming M."

"Em's M. That's funny." When I gave him my best glare, he quickly added, "Doesn't matter. When he got home that night he must have started thinking—thinking is very bad for men. They practically never do it, so when finally they do get to thinking, it's usually with disastrous results."

"You're a man."

"I'm not a man. I'm gay. There's a difference. So he must have started thinking, is this really the woman I want to spend the rest of my life with? Is this really the face I want to see across the breakfast table for the next fifty years? Yes? No? Maybe?" He shrugged. "It's obvious what he decided."

"Ugh," I said in response, then gave Jarrett a punch on the shoulder.

"Hey! What was that for?!"

"For being an ass."

"I'm not an ass. I'm your friend. I'm just laying it all out for you." He rubbed his shoulder. "I bruise easily. You know that. So don't do it again."

"I won't do it again if you stop being an ass."

"I'm not! I'm being your friend. And in return you give me a bruise."

"Ask Deshawn to put some cream on that."

Jarrett's face lit up. "You know? I think I will."

Deshawn Little was Jarrett's fiancé. He'd been Jarrett's manservant, until they discovered they harbored feelings for each other deeper than mere employment allowed. Jarrett had gone down on one knee, and now they were ready to tie the knot. Or not. They were still trying to decide which way they were leaning. The problem was the move from the master-and-servant stage to the equal-under-the-sun stage. It was hard for Deshawn to let go of his subservient manner, and for Jarrett to lose a superb valet.

"Have you found a replacement for Deshawn yet?"

"Not yet. And not for lack of trying, either. We've been interviewing plenty of candidates, but so far no luck. It's very hard to replace the best valet in the world."

"I'm sure you'll find someone."

"I'm not. And neither is Deshawn. I swear, that man's standards are even higher than my own."

"Of course. He knows what the job entails. He knows how hard it is to replace himself."

"Well, I hope he lowers his standards, or else we're never going to agree on a person."

I looked around, thinking we should probably get started on rooting out this pesky ghost. "Buckley?" I asked, looking up. "Are you there?"

Sir Geoffrey Buckley, ever since he'd passed away, had been an integral part of our team. He was the one who usually made contact with the ghosts, seeing as he was one himself, and knew where to find them. Of course, first we had to find Buckley, as he had a habit of floating around the racetrack.

"Buckley!" Jarrett demanded. "Where are you?!"

"Oh, hold on to your butts," a tired voice sounded near the casino bar. A frizzy-haired head popped up, looking slightly disheveled. It belonged to a dapper gentleman dressed in an immaculate suit. The former antique dealer seemed reluctant to join us tonight.

"What happened to you?" Jarrett asked. "Have you been on a bender?"

Buckley gave Jarrett the evil eye. "How can I go on a bender? I'm dead."

"Still. Maybe you found a way."

"No, I didn't find a way. Though I wouldn't mind a snifter. This being dead thing might seem all fine and dandy to you young whippersnappers, but it gets a little tedious after a while."

"We need your help, Buckley," I said. "A man has been killed."

"So what else is new? Men are killed every day. And women, for that matter. And children, dogs, cats, and perfectly nice chunks of rain forest."

Yep, Buckley was in a great mood. "His ghost has been haunting the studio for the past couple of days, and they need him gone."

"It's the new Harry Potter movie, Buckley," Jarrett said encouragingly. "They're finally making another one, isn't that great?"

Buckley shrugged. "Who cares?"

"Well, I do. I've always wondered what Harry was up to these past few years," said Jarrett. "And so have millions of other Harry Potter fans."

Buckley pressed a hand to his head and groaned. He almost sounded like Moaning Myrtle. "If you must know, I did go on a bender, but not an alcoholically induced one. Me and a bunch of other ghosts tried to make our horses go faster, and let me tell you, once you try to take over a horse you start to realize why they've been running races, carrying riders and pulling plows all these years. They're not the most intelligent creatures."

"You... possessed a horse?" I asked, incredulous.

He nodded. "I just figured if a ghost can possess another human, why not a horse? I thought if I could imbibe him with my fighting spirit, I might induce him to win the race. Only problem was that the horse liked me a little too much, and wouldn't let me go! And instead of winning his race he just started prancing around, jumping into the stands like an idiot. Craig Barley had better luck. His horse won, with Frank 'The Stump' Neverlass's lass a close second."

I shook my head and decided I didn't want to know about Buckley's adventures at the Hippodrome. "Do you think you can contact our ghost? We really need to get a move on. We're under contract here, Buckley."

"Yeah, and the police want us out of here, so any excuse will be good to give us the boot," Jarrett added.

Buckley glanced at Darian. "Darian wants you gone? But why?"

"Beats me," I said. "He has a new partner, who told us to take a hike."

Buckley shook his head, and then floated up from behind the bar. I didn't know how he did it, but before long, the ghost of a very large man emerged from the ceiling, where apparently he'd been hiding. He looked exactly like the dead man, which was logical, cause he was the dead man.

"Hey there, buddy," Jarrett said encouragingly. "Mind if we have a chat?"

"He killed me," the man said gloomily. "And Harry Potter couldn't save me."

"Harry Potter can't save anyone," I said. "Because Harry Potter doesn't exist."

"Don't keep saying that," Jarrett hissed. "We're in the temple of Harry Potter here. That's sacrilege. Soon the Dark Lord himself will show up and curse you."

"The Dark Lord!" the dead man cried. "He's the one that did this to me! He has returned!"

I sighed. This was going to be a tough nut to crack. "Uriel Pieres? That's your name, right? Could you tell us what happened? Exactly?"

Uriel floated down from the ceiling and joined us. He seemed to realize he didn't have anything to worry about with us. None of us looked like a creepy dark wizard. "I was cleaning up the casino—they said they were going to shoot a big scene here and needed the place spic and span."

"When was this?" I asked.

"Um…" He frowned. "What day is today?"

"Wednesday."

His face cleared. "Hey, what do you know? It was a week ago."

No wonder his body was smelling to high heaven. If he'd been stuffed up there for a week, it was a miracle they hadn't found him sooner.

"So what happened?"

"Well, I was mopping the floor when a bunch of wizards came in."

"Wizards?"

"The people casting the spells," Jarrett said helpfully. "Harry Potter is a wizard, and so is Ron Weasley. Hermione Granger, on the other hand, is a witch. Because she's a girl. Men are wizards, women are witches. Got it?"

"I know what wizards are," I said. "I just didn't think they existed."

"And that from a woman who believes in ghosts," Jarrett said, raising his eyes to the ceiling.

"That's different. Ghosts are just dead people who can't accept they're dead. Wizards are something some writer invented in an office."

"Just keep telling yourself that," Jarrett said, shaking his head.

"So what did these 'wizards' look like?"

"Well, like wizards," Uriel said helpfully. "You know, with black robes and stuff, and wands. Oh, and they were all wearing masks and pointy hats."

"Wizards," Jarrett said knowingly. "The pointy hats gave them away. And the wands."

"Just a bunch of people dressed up as wizards," I insisted stubbornly.

"I don't think so," Uriel said, his large flabby face contorted into a frown. "I mean, I've worked on all of the Harry Potter movies, and I think I can tell a real wizard from a fake one."

"You worked on the Harry Potter movies?" Jarrett asked. "As a cleaner, you mean?"

"Oh, no. That's just this movie. I was Daniel Radcliffe's butt before."

"His… butt," I said dubiously.

"Yeah. Daniel had qualms about showing his naked butt on the screen, so the producers got him a butt double." He proudly tapped his butt. "Yours truly."

"I don't remember seeing Harry Potter's naked butt in any of the movies," Jarrett said, sounding disappointed.

"That's because the director decided not to use my scenes. Harry was supposed to get a needle prick in the butt in the first movie, when he was holed up in the hospital, and then again in the second movie, but they decided to cut those parts." He gave us a sad face. "They cut *all* my parts."

Yeah, that was what the world wanted to see. Harry Potter's butt. "So let's get back to those wizards," I prompted. "What did they want?"

"That's what I asked them. But then promptly a couple of them grabbed me and held me up. And that's when I saw him." His eyes went wide with fear. "The Dark Lord himself."

"No way!" Jarrett cried excitedly. He was hanging on Uriel's every word.

I groaned inwardly. This was just too ridiculous. Uriel seemed to believe it, though, for he nodded frantically. "He gave a long speech. Something about wanting to take revenge on mortals—that's me—and that I didn't deserve to live." He swallowed, sweat trickling down his ghostly brow as he relived the ghastly scene. "And that's when he cast a curse."

"Avada Kedavra?" Jarrett asked, licking his lips.

Uriel squeezed his eyes tightly shut and shivered at the recollection. "No. It sounded like... Ava Carnivara or something."

"Perhaps a variation," Jarrett said.

"And then what?" I asked.

"And then I died."

I looked at Jarrett. Jarrett looked at me. We both looked at Buckley, who yawned, and then back at Uriel. "You died?" I asked.

"Just like that?" Jarrett added.

"Well, there was a flash of lightning that seemed to leap from the Dark Lord's wand, and a lot of blue light, and the atmosphere crackled and hummed, and there was a roaring crash of thunder, and then... yeah, then I died. Boom. Dropped dead." He sighed. "And then they stuffed my body up there and I've been trying to catch the attention of those bozos over there ever since." He gestured at the three lead actors, who were now being interviewed by Reto Slack. "I liked the original actors a lot better," he said. "These newbies are just plain terrible. Can't act for crap."

"That's what I figured," Jarrett said, darting a glance at the actor who played Harry. He'd taken off his round glasses and actually looked kinda cute. Very muscular and very big. More like Vin Diesel or Dwayne Johnson.

"Yeah, nobody can beat Daniel Radcliffe," Uriel said.

Jarrett grinned. "Great butt, huh?"

Uriel patted his own butt. "The best."

Chapter Three

Uriel drifted off, to go sulk in a corner. Buckley drifted

after him, placed a comforting hand on his shoulder, and proceeded to instruct him on the ins and outs of passing on from this plane and onto the next.

"Buckley is turning into a great death coach," Jarrett said.

"He certainly is."

We wandered over to the producer, who was tapping furiously on her smartphone, probably sending a missive to her own boss about what was going on. When we drifted into her ken, she didn't even look up. "So? Is he gone?"

"I don't think he'll cause you any more trouble," I said.

"That's great. We're behind schedule as it is." Then she looked up and gave us a bright smile. She had a nice smile, and I instantly warmed to her. "Why don't I give you the grand tour? I think you deserve it." She glanced at Jarrett's T-shirt. It depicted the three grinning faces of the original Harry Potter actors when they were kids. "I take it you're a fan."

"Oh, I'm a superfan," Jarrett said. "So why didn't you cast the original actors?"

"Because they're too old?" I said. "Duh. Even I knew that, Jarrett."

"They're not too old. They could easily slip back into their parts."

"It's not because they're too old," Marsha said as she walked us off the Monte Carlo set. "It's because this movie isn't part of the original franchise."

She had Jarrett's attention. "What do you mean?"

"I mean that the studio has no intention to make more Harry Potter movies, or Miss Rowling to write more books, so we decided to jump into the hole they created and make our own trilogy—or quadrilogy, pentalogy or whatever the market demands."

Jarrett looked like a kid who'd been robbed of his lollipop. "So this isn't a JK Rowling sanctioned installment?"

"Nope. Afraid not."

"But how is that even possible?"

"One of the uncredited screenwriters on one of the original movies retained the rights to certain aspects of the storyline—probably a clerical error on the part of the studio, mind you—and decided to approach us with an offer to expand on it, and turn it into a new trilogy. There was some legal wrangling with Warner Brothers and the production company but we finally got the go-ahead from the judge to create a spinoff."

"Rowling mustn't be happy about this."

"She's sore as a gumboil, but at this point she can't prevent us from proceeding. We brought in two screenwriters from the James Bond franchise, and we're taking the Harry Potter universe in a completely different direction."

"What direction?" Jarrett asked suspiciously.

"You'll see. More fun. More action."

He arched an eyebrow. "More explosions? More car chases?"

She smiled. "More of everything." Jarrett winced visibly, but the producer pretended not to notice. "The story will be a retread of *Casino Royale*, which will give us the opportunity to put a new spin on the tired old Harry Potter concept. We will see a grittier Harry, tougher and more world-weary, while he battles both his own demons and those in the real world." She gave Harry a wink. "Are you ready to see Harry emerge from the sea, naked torso and six-pack abs and all?"

"Um..."

"I know I am," said Jarrett, suddenly showing a spark of interest.

"And Harry will have a new love interest, of course," said Marsha. "More than one, in fact. And Harry will finally kiss Hermione, of course."

"He will?" I asked, disappointed. I'd always been on Team Ron.

"You know what would be truly novel and refreshing?" Jarrett asked. "If Harry and Ron got it on. I mean, who wants to see another kissing scene with tired old Hermione?"

"Um, I would," I said, holding up my hand. "I like Ron and Hermione."

"Well, I'd like to see Harry and Ron explore their smoldering passion," he said stubbornly.

"Harry and Ron don't have any smoldering passion."

"They do, too. They just don't want to admit it. Classic."

Marsha laughed. "Maybe we'll keep that for a future movie."

She led us to the next gigantic soundstage, this one where the Hogwarts Great Hall was constructed.

"Wow," I said, properly impressed. It looked just like in the movies, with the long tables where the houses sat, and the dais for the professors.

"Pretty cool, huh?" Marsha said. "This has cost us a fortune to recreate. Too bad we'll have to demolish it."

"Demolish it?" Jarrett asked, aghast.

"Yeah, the bad guy—Frank Riddle—is going to take it out with a missile attack. It's going to be the opening of our movie. Great, big set piece."

"Missile? What about magic?" Jarrett asked.

"Nope. No magic in this movie. Rowling owns the right to the magic."

"No magic?" asked Jarrett, his voice a squeak.

"That's right. No magic. This will be a non-magic Harry Potter."

Jarrett gave me a look of despair and I shook my head. A lot of people were going to be disappointed in the new and improved Potter.

The producer led us to the next soundstage, this one

where the interior shots of Hogwarts would be taken. The common room. The hallways. The classrooms. Jarrett was perking up again. "Now this is more like it. So Harry is going back to Hogwarts?"

Marsha gave him a frown. "Harry and the others graduated, Jarrett. You as a superfan should know that. No, we're just going to use these sets to show a new generation being trained as witches and wizards, only to gruesomely die in the attack on the castle." She waved her hand like a wand. "All these sets will be turned to rubble. It's going to be awesome. When Harry stands on the ruins, his robe billowing around his bare thighs, he swears a solemn oath to avenge the deaths of these young witches and wizards, and thus the battle begins. Pretty awesome, huh?"

"Very," Jarrett said, eyes glittering. I wondered if he was thinking about Harry's bare thighs or the disaster this movie would turn out to be.

ABOUT NIC

Nic Saint is the pen name for writing couple Nick and Nicole Saint. They've penned 70+ novels in the romance, cat sleuth, middle grade, suspense, comedy and cozy mystery genres. Nicole has a background in accounting and Nick in political science and before being struck by the writing bug the Saints worked odd jobs around the world (including massage therapist in Mexico, gardener in Italy, restaurant manager in India, and Berlitz teacher in Belgium).

When they're not writing they enjoy Christmas-themed Hallmark movies (whether it's Christmas or not), all manner of pastry, comic books, a daily dose of yoga (to limber up those limbs), and spoiling their big red tomcat Tommy.

Sign up for the no-spam newsletter and be the first to know when a new book comes out: nicsaint.com/newsletter.

www.nicsaint.com

facebook.com/nicsaintauthor

twitter.com/nicsaintauthor

bookbub.com/authors/nic-saint

amazon.com/author/nicsaint

ALSO BY NIC SAINT

Ghosts of London

Between a Ghost and a Spooky Place

Public Ghost Number One

Ghost Save the Queen

Box Set 1 (Books 1-3)

A Tale of Two Harrys

Ghost of Girlband Past

Ghostlier Things

Charleneland

Deadly Ride

Final Ride

Neighborhood Witch Committee

Witchy Start

Witchy Worries

Witchy Wishes

Saffron Diffley

Crime and Retribution

Vice and Verdict

The B-Team

Once Upon a Spy

Tate-à-Tate

Enemy of the Tates

Ghosts vs. Spies

The Ghost Who Came in from the Cold

Witchy Fingers

Witchy Trouble

Witchy Hexations

Witchy Possessions

Witchy Riches

Box Set 1 (Books 1-4)

The Mysteries of Bell & Whitehouse

One Spoonful of Trouble

Two Scoops of Murder

Three Shots of Disaster

Box Set 1 (Books 1-3)

A Twist of Wraith

A Touch of Ghost

A Clash of Spooks

Box Set 2 (Books 4-6)

The Stuffing of Nightmares

A Breath of Dead Air

An Act of Hodd

Box Set 3 (Books 7-9)

Standalone Novels

When in Bruges

The Whiskered Spy

ThrillFix

Homejacking

The Eighth Billionaire

The Wrong Woman

Short Stories

Felonies and Penalties (Saffron Diffley Short 1)

Purrfect Santa (Mysteries of Max Short 1)

Purrfect Christmas Mystery (Mysteries of Max Short 2)

Purrfect Christmas Miracle (Mysteries of Max Short 3)

Purrfectly Flealess (Mysteries of Max Short 4)

Made in the
USA
Monee, IL